God has brought me this far; why would He let me down now?

She tried to convince herself, but the familiar saying merely mocked her frustration.

Sarah heard footsteps behind her and decided to ignore them until a familiar voice said, "May I give you a lift?" Ryder matched strides with her. "There's no reason to freeze waiting for the shuttle when I'm going through town myself."

Sarah shuddered in the cold as she shook her head. The offer was tempting, but she'd been able to keep her double life a secret from her classmates for over eighteen months and she still felt she wasn't ready to explain her daily visits to the "Little Lambs Children's Center." She had a great deal of respect for Ryder and she didn't want her past to come between their casual friendship. Nearly three years before, Sarah had vowed that she would never again become interested in men. However, since she entered college she was beginning to find it more and more difficult to keep that vow.

ANN BELL is a librarian by profession and lives in Iowa with her husband, Jim, who is her biggest supporter. Ann has worked as a librarian and teacher in Iowa, Oregon, Guam, and Montana. She has been honored in the top three picks of Heartsong members' favorite authors. Her Heartsong books—to this date—all center around a fictional town in Montana called Rocky Bluff. She has also written numerous articles for Christian magazines and a book titled *Proving Yourself: A Study of James.*

Books by Ann Bell

HEARTSONG PRESENTS
HP66—Autumn Love
HP89—Contagious Love
HP109—Inspired Love
HP137—Distant Love
HP153—Healing Love
HP193—Compassionate Love
HP317—Love Remembered

Love
Abounds

Ann Bell

Heartsong Presents

Dedicated to those who live with the day-to-day challenges of genetic birth defects, especially Judy Sagal, an avid reader of Heartsong Presents. Judy is one of the oldest survivors with spina bifida and is a source of encouragement and strength to others with disabilities and their parents and caregivers.

A note from the author:
I love to hear from my readers! You may correspond with me by writing:
Ann Bell
Author Relations
PO Box 719
Uhrichsville, OH 44683

ISBN 1-57748-982-9

LOVE ABOUNDS

Cover illustration by Kay Salem.

one

Sarah Brown dropped the letter onto her desk as her tearful eyes drifted listlessly through the window toward the administration building of Rocky Bluff Community College. The grass was a brittle brown while the leaves lay in piles against the surrounding structures. Generally, there would have been at least one major snowfall in central Montana before Thanksgiving, but this had been an exceptionally warm autumn and the strongest leaves were still clinging tenaciously to the trees. Her term paper was due the following week, she had a group presentation consisting of a debate before the entire class on their selected topic, plus final exams were two weeks away.

Why does this have to happen to me now? She groaned with frustration as a lump built in her throat. *In spite of how hard I've worked, it looks as if I'll have to drop out of school and work two jobs until I can save enough money to finish. My financial aid for next semester is only going to be enough to cover my tuition and books, and not nearly enough to cover my room and board. As much as I hate to do it, I suppose I'd better go talk to my advisor tomorrow and let him know that I won't be back for spring semester.*

A shrill ring interrupted Sarah's worries. She reached for the telephone on the corner of her desk. "Hello."

"Hello, Sarah," a cheerful baritone voice greeted. "I thought you were going to meet with our debate team at the library at two o'clock." A slight tease resonated in his voice. "We can't function here without you."

Sarah glanced at the clock over her roommate's dresser and gasped. "Oh no. I forgot all about it. I'll get my notes and be right over."

"Great. We'll be waiting for you in the corner study room on the main floor."

Sarah nearly ran the entire way across campus to the library. When she breathlessly arrived five minutes later, three of her classmates were already clustered around a rectangular table, engaged in heavy debate.

"Glad you could join us," Ryder Long scolded jovially as he pulled out the chair next to him for her. "We're in the process of deciding who will take the affirmative position in support of the United States' involvement in the building of the International Space Station and who will argue against it. So far, we have two in favor of the project and one uncommitted. How do you stand?"

Sarah took her seat and glanced around the table at her classmates. As much as she liked each one of them, she would much rather work on a project independently. Although collaboration was considered an extremely effective educational tool, Sarah often felt as if they were designing an elephant by committee instead of planning a usable presentation. However, in spite of her misgiving, she immediately joined into the group dynamics. "I've been doing a lot of research over the Internet about the ISS, and from what I've learned, I think our country would be much farther ahead spending our tax money on social services instead of more hardware toys for the scientists," she stated firmly.

"Spoken like a true liberal," Ryder teased.

Sarah's face reddened as she tried to maintain her composure. "My viewpoint has nothing to do with my politics," she retorted sharply. "But it has a lot to do with my own personal experiences. I don't like to see some people have extra while others starve and can't pay their bills."

Marcella Cross's eyes widened and an expression of concern spread across her face. "How are you in more pain than the rest of us?" she queried sarcastically. "Aren't we all in this college struggle together?"

Sarah studied her friend's innocent face and trendy clothing. Sarah rarely shared her background with her classmates because most would not understand the hurtful, complex events that had brought her to Rocky Bluff to attend college. Knowing that she could only tell part of the story, Sarah took a deep breath and replied, "For one thing, I just learned that my financial aid for next semester won't be enough to cover my room and board, so I'll have to drop out of school until I can save enough money to finish. If more money were available for education, I'd be able to graduate this spring with everyone else."

A shocked look spread across each of her classmates' faces. She knew that those who were able to live at home with their parents had little understanding of the pressures of those who had to pay for their own room and board.

"Surely there's some way you can stay in school," Ryder responded sympathetically. "I'd hate to think that you got within five months of graduation and then weren't able to finish your associate's degree. You're one of the hardest workers in our class."

Sarah fixed her eyes. "Don't worry. . .I'll be back," she promised. "I have a better motivator to complete my degree and get a good paying job than most students." Before anyone could question her further, Sarah immediately changed the subject. "Now back to the space station question. . .How are we going to proceed with our debate? It looks like whoever is undecided will need to argue against the U.S. involvement in the International Space Station with me. He or she can supply the objective facts, and I'll supply the passion."

Everyone nodded in agreement. "That settles the easy part," Ryder shrugged. "Now for the hard part—how can we obtain enough documentation to substantiate our individual viewpoints?"

The other team members looked at each other with blank stares and shrugged their shoulders as Sarah shuffled through her papers. "I found a fantastic Webquest on the Internet that was put together by a high school principal in Brazil and a high school media specialist in Iowa. It contains links to all kinds of Internet sites pertaining to the International Space Station and it's organized by how each group with a vested interest in the space station views the need for this project."

❧

As Sarah spoke, Ryder studied Sarah's delicate features and strong determination. There was something mysteriously different about her. She was not only highly intelligent and highly motivated, but the intensity in her eyes portrayed an aura of mystery that none of her peers possessed. "At least one person has done her homework," he said with a smile as the others glanced ashamedly at the floor. "Could you tell us the Internet address so we can all take a look at it?"

"Just a second," Sarah muttered as the others took out their pencils and waited while she shuffled through her notebook. "Here it is," she replied after a long pause. "http//www. camanche.k12.ia.us/webquest."

"Has anyone else done any research on the topic?" Ryder asked as his eyes went from Marcella to Josh. "We can't expect Sarah to do all the work." Both shook their heads as their faces flushed with embarrassment.

This collaborative group project was developing the same way that most of the other groups that Sarah had been involved with had gone. The faces were different, but the roles people played were always the same. First, there was the self-appointed leader—in this case, it was Ryder. The leader's position was generally not based on ability, but on personal assertiveness. Generally, the leader did not have to work so hard as the others because he had the talent of motivating others. There often seemed to be at least one person who was either too busy or too lazy to carry his share of the assignment, offset by one overachiever who was willing to do the majority of the work in order to receive the highest grade possible. Sarah smiled to herself as she realized that she was once again playing the role of the overachiever. She often wished that she would not become so emotionally involved in her studies, but she seemed not to be able to control herself. She occasionally laughed about this trait's being an obsessive-compulsive disorder.

Ryder leaned back in his chair. "Sarah has already done her homework," he declared as he maintained his role of group leader. "Can everyone meet here tomorrow at four o'clock to begin putting this thing together? Time is beginning to run out on us."

"Fine by me," Marcella agreed, knowing that she had a date with one of the football players and would probably not be home until late.

"I think I can make it," Josh nodded.

Sarah's eyes drifted from person to person, as her spirits dropped. "I hate being a spoilsport," she said softly, sensing their potential disapproval, "but I have a commitment every day at four. Could we meet a little earlier?"

Josh Richardson shook his head while he gave a frustrated sigh. "I don't get off work at the student union until three, but you could start without me. I could probably be here by three fifteen at the latest."

Everyone looked at Ryder for his approval. "Then let's

meet at three and Josh can join us as soon as he can," he said authoritatively. The others nodded with agreement without noticing the pained expression spreading across Sarah's face. One by one, the foursome put on their coats, gathered their books, said farewell, and left.

Sarah's sense of isolation followed her outside where a sharp northerly wind ruffled her light-brown hair. *I wonder how long it will take me to save enough money to come back to college,* she mused as she walked the two blocks to the nearest bus stop as she had done nearly every day at this time since she'd been in Rocky Bluff. She had the schedule of the shuttle between the small campus and the downtown memorized—every half-hour until six o'clock and once an hour between six and midnight.

God has brought me this far; why would He let me down now? She tried to convince herself, but the familiar saying merely mocked her frustration.

Sarah heard footsteps behind her and decided to ignore them until a familiar voice said, "May I give you a lift?" Ryder matched strides with her. "There's no reason to freeze waiting for the shuttle when I'm going through town myself."

Sarah shuddered in the cold as she shook her head. The offer was tempting, but she'd been able to keep her double life a secret from her classmates for over eighteen months and she still felt she wasn't ready to explain her daily visits to the "Little Lambs Children's Center." She had a great deal of respect for Ryder and she didn't want her past to come between their casual friendship. Nearly three years before, Sarah had vowed that she would never again become interested in men. However, since she entered college she was beginning to find it more and more difficult to keep that vow.

After a few moments of contemplation, Sarah turned her attention back to Ryder. "Thanks for the offer," she responded graciously, "but I don't want to be an inconvenience. The bus should be along within five minutes."

≈

Ryder's shoulders slumped. He had met Sarah during freshman orientation and was immediately impressed with her enthusiasm toward learning. Yet, an aura of painful mystery seemed always to surround her and he was not able to find a way to break through her aloof exterior. "Whenever you need a ride and the bus is late, just give me a call," he said as he placed his arm on her shoulder. "In the meantime, I'll see you tomorrow at three. Don't work too hard on the project tonight. Make the others do their share."

"Don't worry about that," Sarah smiled as she sat down on the edge of the bench at the bus stop. She watched as Ryder strolled confidently toward the parking lot. His thick jet-black hair fell smoothly to his shoulders characteristic of many of the Native Americans in the area. Sarah had often seen Ryder Long in church, plus he had been in several of her classes during the last two semesters. She was impressed with his work ethic and drive for success. He never seemed to be lacking for friends and was the first one to greet a new student and welcome him to the campus. *If I had come to college strictly to meet guys, Ryder would be one of the first ones I'd check out,* Sarah sighed, *but I have to accept the fact that my life will never follow a traditional pattern of education, job, marriage, and then a family.*

Just then, the shuttle pulled to a stop and the door slid open. Sarah showed the driver her pass and took a seat near the front. She blankly watched the rows of ranch style homes fly past the window. Until she received the letter about her student aid, she thought she had her future well planned, but now fears and uncertainties enveloped her. What would the future hold for her and her daughter if she had to drop out of college?

Twenty minutes later, Sarah stepped from the city shuttle and walked the two blocks to Little Lambs Children's Center. The building was once the center for most of the medical care in Rocky Bluff, but when Doctor Brewer retired nearly three years before, the building was converted to a foster home for children with severe birth defects. Sarah still marveled at the seemingly miraculous series of events that led Dawn Harkness Reynolds and her husband, Ryan, to become directors of the home. They both sacrificed well-paying careers to return to Rocky Bluff to care for helpless, needy babies.

Dawn had been a successful obstetrics nurse in Billings when she became reacquainted with Ryan Reynolds, an old schoolmate from Rocky Bluff. Their common heritage added fuel to their smoldering romance. Soon after they were married, the opportunity to return to their hometown to help establish the "Little Lambs Children's Center" presented itself and neither one could resist. Both had been active in the Right-to-Life Movement and felt a deep desire to help both mothers and their disabled children. In the last three years, the home had cared for over thirty babies and had trained ten of the mothers to care for their own child so that they could accept full custodial care. Sarah longed for the day that she, too, would be able to take her child home with her.

Upon arriving at the center, Sarah rang the bell and waited. Within a few minutes, a tall blond cradling an infant in her arms opened the door. "Sarah," Dawn Reynolds greeted. "It's good to see you again. Do come in."

Sarah stepped inside and stomped the dust from her shoes. "Charity is still napping," Dawn explained, "but help yourself to a soda in the lounge and join me in the playroom. One of the assistants is sick today so I'm having to cover for her."

Sarah hung her coat on the rack in the lounge and decided against a soft drink. She tiptoed into the small room next door containing four toddler beds. She bent over the one in the far corner and admired the sleeping child. An angelic expression covered the little girl's face. Sarah smiled as she noted how the child's hair was now almost long enough to conceal the shunt that drained the excess fluid from her head to reduce the pressure on her brain. Sarah longed to cuddle Charity in her arms, but did not want to interrupt such a peaceful sleep. Instead, Sarah joined Dawn in the playroom.

Dawn motioned Sarah to take the chair beside her as she continued rocking the infant in her arms. "How was your day?" Dawn asked with a smile.

"Not good," Sarah sighed. "I received some bad news in the mail. . . . I'm afraid I'll have to drop out of school next semester."

Dawn's forehead wrinkled as her mouth dropped. She knew how Sarah had worked and how far she had come in a short time. "What happened?" she queried.

"I got a notice that they will be cutting my financial aid and it will barely be enough to cover my tuition and books," Sarah replied sadly. "Until I finish my training, there is no way I can make enough at a part-time job to pay for my room and board. Tomorrow I'm going to have to tell my advisor that I'm dropping out."

Dawn hesitated. There had to be a way for Sarah to obtain enough money to pay for her room and board for just one more semester. She remembered how four years ago her church in Billings had rallied to help Sarah as an unwed mother who had been disowned by her family. Because of their love and encouragement, Sarah felt the guilt of what she had done and soon accepted Christ's love and forgiveness. In spite of their youth, both Sarah and Jeff Blair, the father, accepted the responsibility for their child born with severe spina bifida and were determined to do whatever necessary to see that she lived as productive a life as possible.

"I hate to see you drop out," Dawn replied. "Let's give it a few more days and see what might turn up. What is the last possible day you can let them know if you will be returning for spring semester?"

Sarah shrugged her shoulders. "We have to register for classes December eleventh, then we have Christmas vacation from the fifteenth to the third of January. There are so few good paying jobs here in Rocky Bluff, that I'll probably have to go job hunting in Billings during vacation time."

"If you move back to Billings you won't be able to see Charity every day and you'll postpone your biggest goal of all—that of being a self-supporting, custodial parent," Dawn reminded her.

❧

Sarah continued rocking silently. Her eyes studied the designs in the tile. She knew how true Dawn's words were, but could she muster enough faith to believe that somewhere out there, God had a solution to her problem? Suddenly, her thoughts were interrupted by a familiar cry from the adjoining room, "Want up. Want up."

Sarah hurried to her daughter's bedside. Charity's face brightened as her mother leaned over to pick her up. The child's legs hung limply from her torso. The opening of the spinal column that was closed soon after her birth was just below her armpit and Charity had no feeling or movement below that level.

"Hi, Mommy," she greeted. "Want dolly."

Sarah smiled as she hugged her daughter and leaned over to fetch the Raggedy Ann doll in the corner of the bed. She had purchased the stuffed doll at the local discount store and had given it to Charity for her second birthday. Since that time, Charity and Raggedy Ann had been inseparable, and Sarah had taken pride in selecting a toy that would meet her daughter's need to cuddle. Little by little Sarah was learning how to care for her daughter and her goal was to have total custody of Charity by the child's fifth birthday. At that time, she hoped to have completed her associate's degree as a computer technician and obtained a good-paying job.

Sarah carried her daughter into the playroom and took Charity's favorite storybook from the shelf. Returning to the rocking chair beside Dawn, Sarah quietly read the all-too-familiar tale to her daughter. After completing the book, the young mother picked up a plastic game board and began pointing to each of the primary colors and saying its name slowly. Charity was quick to imitate her mother's sounds and was beginning to make the association between the color and its name.

After at least fifteen minutes of providing undivided attention to her daughter, Sarah turned to the director of the center. "Dawn, it's amazing how many words she's learned. I may be prejudiced, but Charity seems to be smarter than any of the other kids here."

Dawn smiled at the young mother's innocent pride. They had been monitoring the child's language development to help determine if there had been any brain damage from the hydrocephalus, but so far, Charity's language skills were average for her age group. "The specialists have been extremely pleased with her development," Dawn assured her. "Tomorrow her occupational therapist will be here at two o'clock. Would you be able to come a little early and be here when she works with Charity? She'll be able to answer more of your questions about her development."

Sarah took a deep breath. "I promised my study group I'd meet with them at three o'clock tomorrow to work on a boring debate about the International Space Station. I don't know what to do. I've got to get a good grade in my political science class, but I also want to be a good mother to Charity."

Dawn patted Sarah on the arm. "Don't put a guilt trip on yourself," she reminded her. "If you don't see the therapist tomorrow she'll be here again next week. Maybe she'll have even more details for you then."

Sarah nodded her head. "I know," she sighed, "but I'd really like to talk with her as soon as possible. I'll make some phone calls tonight and see what I can do."

Dawn laid the child she was holding on the play mat, excused herself, and went to the kitchen to check the progress of the evening meal. Sarah laid Charity on the mat on the opposite corner. In the center of the mat was an assortment of toddler toys. The two children began scooting toward the toys, pulling with their arms and dragging their limp legs behind them. Sarah watched with amazement. Even though neither one had feeling nor movement below the waist, they both were learning to adapt to their limitations and overcome them.

Sarah's eyes widened as she glanced at her watch. She hurried to the kitchen door and caught Dawn's attention while she was checking the day's shopping list. "Time got away from me again," she said with a smile. "I'm going to have to run so I can catch the five o'clock shuttle back to the campus. I'll see you tomorrow."

"Bye now," Dawn shouted as Sarah hurried out the door.

two

Sarah Brown thumbed through the student directory. Her hands trembled. She hated to ask a favor of a man, but he had offered her a ride any time she needed one and this time her desire to meet with the occupational therapist outweighed her embarrassment about asking for a favor. There it was on page ten. Ryder Long: 259-8157. She took a deep breath and then dialed the numbers.

"Hello."

"Hello. Is Ryder Long available, please?" Sarah asked, her voice trembling.

"This is he."

"Hello, Ryder. This is Sarah Brown. I hate to bother you, but I have a favor to ask of you."

Ryder stretched out his long legs, muted the TV, and leaned back on the sofa. "Hi, Sarah. I'm glad you called. I was getting kind of bored tonight and needed someone to talk to."

Sarah hesitated, she wanted to hang up but the face of her daughter flashed before her. "Ryder, earlier today you mentioned that if I ever needed a ride to give you a call. . . . Well, I do have a need for a ride. . .that is. . .if it wouldn't be too inconvenient for you."

"Nothing for you would be too inconvenient," Ryder laughed. "When can I come and get you?"

"Are you busy between two thirty and three o'clock tomorrow afternoon?" Sarah asked hesitantly. "I have an appointment at two o'clock downtown, but if I wait for the shuttle I

17

might not make it back for our group meeting at three."

Ryder smiled. This was the first time Sarah had spoken to him about anything that wasn't related to their class work. He hoped that maybe this would be the time he could get past her mysterious exterior. "That's no problem at all," he assured her. "I have to come through downtown on my way to the campus anyway. Where would you like me to meet you?"

Sarah knew the moment of truth had come. She'd at least have to tell a portion of her secret. Fortunately, Ryder seemed to be the type who would accept her just the way she was, without prying into her background. "I'll be at the Little Lambs Children's Center. Do you know where that is?"

Ryder wrinkled his forehead. "I've lived in Rocky Bluff all my life, but I've never heard of The Little Lambs. Where is it?"

"In the 600 block of Dodge Street. . .where Doctor Brewer's office used to be. They remodeled the building after he retired three years ago."

"I spent a lot of unhappy hours in that office," Ryder chuckled, remembering all his childhood diseases and injuries. "So they changed it into a day care center, huh?"

Sarah gulped. "Not exactly. . .it's a foster home for children who are born with spina bifida and other such birth defects."

"Sounds interesting. . . Are you working there part-time, or something?"

"Well. . .er. . .not exactly. . . It's more like volunteer work."

Ryder could not miss the hesitation in her voice. "Sorry, I didn't mean to sound like I was prying. I think that's a noble project to be connected with. Maybe I should do some community service there as well."

Sarah's fingers tightened around the phone as her face

blanched. "Yeah. . . You'll have to give them a call some-time. . . . See you tomorrow."

"I'll be there at ten of three tomorrow," Ryder promised. "In the meantime, I have a lot of research to do on the space station. It wouldn't be fair if you had to do all the work."

Sarah said good-bye, hung up the phone, and buried her head in her hands. She wanted to become an advocate for children with disabilities, but she knew that if she did, she would be forced to tell her long-held secret. Deciding to continue masking her heartache and pain, Sarah took her coat from the hook behind the door and headed toward the computer lab in the next building. There she could immerse herself in the development of a detailed spreadsheet, while she pushed her fears to the far crevices of her mind.

Most of the other students owned their own computers, but Sarah felt fortunate just to receive financial aid to cover her tuition and room and board and could only dream of the day when she would own her own computer. Ever since she had returned to high school after the birth of little Charity, Sarah had become fascinated with hardware and systems components of computers. While most of the girls seemed interested only in word processing and simple graphics, Sarah sat side by side with the computer nerds learning about the computer's inner components, and how to install programs, networks, and all the peripheral devices.

Now, just when she was just one semester from completing the course, the government was cutting back on her financial aid. She was determined not to worry about it until after she took her last test of the semester, but, in spite of her best efforts, her fears continued to haunt her. If she had to drop out of college she wanted to make sure her grades would be good enough so that when she returned she could pick up exactly where she left off. What troubled her most was the realization of how fast technology was changing and if she had to interrupt her education for just six months, she would be put several years behind.

While Sarah was peering into a monitor in the back of the lab, her troubles began to fade. The challenge of figuring out how to manipulate the numbers with a simple click of a mouse served as a needed distraction to make the hours fly. Sarah's reputation as one of the more knowledgeable students in the field spread rapidly. Every time she was in the computer lab, she was usually interrupted several times by questions from other students. She thrived on keeping her personal relationships on an academic and polite level, but occasionally she felt the walls begin to crumble. Whenever she was with Ryder Long, she found it harder and harder to maintain her aloof, intellectual façade.

❧

At 2:45 the next day, Ryder Long stopped his green sports car in front of the large, brick, one-story building on Dodge Street. His curiosity was further piqued by the sign:

Little Lambs Children's Center
Montana Home and Education Center
For Children with Birth Defects
Directors: Ryan Reynolds and Dawn Reynolds

Could the director be the same Ryan Reynolds that was my sports idol in grade school? Ryder wondered. *It's hard to imagine a high school jock specializing in handicapped children, instead of becoming a coach somewhere, but the chance of someone else with that name turning up in Rocky Bluff seems remote.*

As Ryder sat immersed in thought, Sarah emerged from the front entrance and hurried toward the waiting car. "Hi,

Ryder. I hope I didn't keep you waiting," she greeted as she opened the passenger door and joined her classmate.

"You're right on time," the young man assured her as he started the engine. "I was a couple of minutes early."

Sarah shuffled nervously. This was the closest she wanted anyone in school to come to her secret. "I sure appreciate your giving me a ride. If there's ever a favor I can do for you just let me know."

"The next time my hard drive crashes, you'll be the first one I'll call," Ryder laughed. He then paused as a serious expression spread across his face. "While I was waiting I noticed on the sign that Ryan Reynolds was one of the directors. Do you happen to know where he went to high school? Was it here in Rocky Bluff?"

"Yes, he grew up here and, like most of the others, he left soon after graduation to get an education," Sarah explained cautiously, wondering where the conversation was heading. "When I first met him he was selling medical supplies."

Ryder turned onto the street toward the campus and drove in silence for a few blocks. "That's interesting," he replied thoughtfully. "I wonder what got him interested in disabled children. . . . I remember him as one of the best athletes in high school and wouldn't have been at all surprised if he had ended up coaching a university football team."

"People do change," Sarah replied, thinking more of her own situation than Ryan's. "All I know is that he'd been involved in the Montana Right-to-Life Movement for some time and when he married Dawn Harkness they returned to Rocky Bluff and helped start Little Lambs."

Ryder couldn't hold back his fond memories and began laughing. "Don't tell me he married the daughter of the man that used to run the hardware store? She was some beauty. I think she was even the homecoming queen one year. Every boy in the third grade had a crush on her when she was in high school."

Little by little, Sarah relaxed. Maybe Ryder could be someone she could trust after all. Campus life had become extremely lonely for her as she tried to keep the most important part of her life a secret. "Dawn is still beautiful," Sarah replied, "only now in a much different way. I don't know where I'd be without her."

"I'd like to meet her again sometime," Ryder said as he turned into the main gate of the campus. "I'm always fascinated with the different paths the people of Rocky Bluff take; yet, they always seem to maintain an allegiance to this little town."

Ryder found a parking spot in the second row from the main entrance to the library. They sprang from the car, rushed into the library toward the study room on the main floor. Marcella was already waiting, her fingers tapping the table with impatience.

"Sorry we're late," Ryder gasped, as he took off his coat and threw it on the chair next to him. "I hope you haven't been waiting long."

"I got out early from my last class," she explained, "so I came directly to the library. I have to meet my folks at four thirty, so I hope we can finish this project in a hurry."

Just then, Josh rushed into the library study room. Everyone nodded and muttered greetings to each other. Ryder took out his notebook in his typical authoritarian manner. "Here's a list of Internet sites that I found on the International Space Station. I starred the ones that support the U.S. involvement and wrote a brief summary on each site. I could take everyone's lists to the copier so all of us have the same sources."

"Good idea," Josh agreed, reaching into his backpack for his notes.

Sarah handed Ryder three pages of detailed notes, while Marcella's were a half-page long. Ryder frowned as he perused her abbreviated list.

"Sorry," she shrugged. "I was extra busy last night and didn't have much time to work on this."

Ryder rolled his eyes and headed to the copier machine. During the next forty-five minutes, the group busily summarized and discussed their main points. When they were finally satisfied that they were organized enough to conduct a reasonable debate before their class, the foursome said good-bye to each other and went their separate ways.

The cold November wind whipped through Sarah's long brown hair as she walked slowly toward her dormitory. An aura of sadness enveloped her. She had trouble imagining that she only had a few more weeks left at Rocky Bluff Community College before she would be working again full-time. Her job would not be in her dreamed profession, but probably at another fast food restaurant. The thought of Ryder's laughing eyes and shining dark hair should have made her smile, but instead it sunk her deeper into depression. *Just when I think I've met someone I can trust, it looks like I'm going to have to drop out of school and probably not see him again,* she mused as she kicked a pile of leaves on the sidewalk. *Oh, well. . .it's probably better to stop a relationship before it even gets started. It would only lead to more heartache, anyway. . .besides, who would want a friend who is the single parent of a disabled child? I might as well accept the harsh, cruel facts and go see my advisor tomorrow and let him know I'm dropping out of school.*

❧

The next day Sarah Brown was done with classes by noon and made an appointment to see her advisor, Jay Harkness, at two o'clock. Mr. Harkness was not only Sarah's college advisor, but she had taken at least two computer classes a semester from him. One of the many things that had attracted her to Rocky Bluff Community College was the fact that Dawn Reynolds's brother was head of the department in which she wanted to major. The more she had studied under him, the more impressed she had become, not only with his intellectual background, but also with his concern for the future of each of his students.

Sarah remembered how proudly Dawn had told her about what a good college instructor her brother was. He had received his bachelor's degree from Montana Tech, and then obtained his master's degree and most of his computer training while he was in the Air Force stationed on Guam. Since returning to Montana, he went to as many workshops and training sessions as possible in order to stay on the cutting edge of a fast-changing industry. All this had made him one of the most well-respected professors on campus.

Promptly at two o'clock, Sarah timidly approached Mr. Harkness's office. When she reached the open door, the prematurely graying professor looked up from his computer screen and smiled. "Come in, Sarah, and have a chair. It's good to see you again."

Sarah smiled as she took the chair beside her advisor's desk. "Thanks for seeing me on such short notice," she whispered as she clutched her purse nervously in her lap.

"That's what I'm here for," Jay assured her as he studied the deep furrows in her forehead. "You look troubled. Is there something I can do to help?"

Sarah hesitated and took a deep breath. "I'm afraid I'm not going to be able to come back to school next semester," she replied sadly as a lump began to grow in her throat.

Jay's eyes widened with disapproval. "Why is that?" he queried. "You've been on the dean's list every semester you've been here, and you only have one semester until you receive your degree."

"I know," she replied as she gazed at the floor. "I hate the thought of dropping out when the end is almost in sight, but I don't have any other alternative. I just learned that my financial aid is being cut and it will only be enough to cover my tuition and books for next semester, and not my room and board. The only option that I can come up with is to drop out of school, return to Billings where I could live with my mother, and save enough money so that I can finish school later."

Jay shook his head. "I'd hate to see that happen. There has to be a way for you to earn your room and board for five months here in Rocky Bluff."

Sarah sat in silence as a smile gradually spread across Jay's face. He reached for the telephone. "I have an idea. It's a long shot, but maybe something can be worked out so that you can remain in school."

Sarah watched her advisor with puzzlement as he checked the phone book and then dialed.

❧

"Hello, Pastor," Jay greeted as Pastor Olson answered his office phone in the church. "This is Jay Harkness. I hope I didn't catch you at a bad time."

"I was just working on Sunday's sermon. What can I do for you?"

"I have a student who will need room and board for next semester, and I was wondering if they have found anyone to stay with Rebecca Hatfield, yet." Jay asked, as he remembered the health care needs of a friend and coworker of his grandmother's.

Rebecca had been the librarian of Rocky Bluff High School while Jay and Dawn Harkness were students. When she retired, she went to Guam for two years to help automate a school library there at the same time that Jay was there on a military assignment to Andersen Air Force Base on the northern tip of the island. Having someone from his hometown there helped ease his homesickness during his first months of duty. Before Rebecca returned to Montana, she introduced Jay to one of her students, Angie Quinata. When Jay was discharged from the service, the two were married and established their first home in Rocky Bluff. Angie quickly fell in love with Montana, in spite of the drastic change of climate from her tropical homeland, and invited her mother to move to Rocky Bluff when she retired from teaching.

Like Jay's grandmother, Edith Harkness Dutton, Rebecca also had found love and fulfillment in a late-in-life marriage. Upon returning to Rocky Bluff, Rebecca married retired Fire Chief Andy Hatfield, and the couple spent ten happy years together volunteering for all types of community and church activities. However, the last few months of Andy's life had been extremely difficult for the aging couple. Rebecca was beginning to exhibit symptoms of the first stages of Alzheimer's disease. Andy had lovingly cared for her and had seen that she had the best medical care possible. And since the Hatfields did not have a family, Andy had arranged for attorney David Wood to be responsible for Rebecca's affairs if something should happen to him.

Then three weeks ago, the entire community mourned the loss of one of their leading citizens, Andy Hatfield. He had suffered a heart attack while mowing his lawn. Friends and church members rallied to Rebecca's support, offering to help her maintain as independent a lifestyle as possible for as long she was capable. Social services arranged for daily home health care and different women from her church took turns spending the night with Rebecca until permanent arrangements could be made.

Pastor Olson was assisting in the search for a permanent, live-in caregiver, but to no avail. He had never thought of the possibility of using a college student. He leaned back in his study chair as he pondered Jay's suggestion. "That's a good idea. I'll have to contact Dave Wood to find out what the status is of Rebecca's home health care needs. Who is the student?"

"Sarah Brown is looking for a situation where she could work for her room and board," Jay explained. "I thought that possibly some arrangements could be worked out between the two of them."

"Umm. . .interesting thought," Pastor Olson replied. "I'll give Dave Wood a call and get back to you as soon as I know something."

The phone conversation ended and Jay turned back to Sarah who was listening with amazement. She had never met the Hatfields but had heard many prayer requests for them when she was in church. "Obviously, I don't know the details, but would you be interested in staying with Rebecca Hatfield and helping her with minor household chores in the evening in exchange for your room and board? Home health care services will help during the daytime, but she needs someone to be with her at night."

Sarah smiled as she breathed a sigh of relief. "I'd be willing to do whatever is necessary in order to finish school."

"Good. . .I'll give you a call as soon as I learn something," Jay replied. "Don't give up hope. I'm sure we can get something worked out for you."

Sarah's return walk across campus was brisker and her steps lighter than they had been in days. God had helped her through many difficult situations and now her faith was again being restored that He was still directing her life through extremely difficult circumstances.

three

Political Science 101 was the liveliest it had been all semester as four students emotionally debated their views concerning the United States Involvement in the International Space Station Project. Sarah Brown led the way in strongly defending the position to spend the billions of dollars now used on the ISS on human services; although Josh supported her, he contributed very little and only seemed to be there to boost her morale. Ryder Long tried to persuade the class that the space station was necessary for national security and scientific research, as Marcella Cross looked on with little to add.

Although Ryder's arguments were strong, Sarah's passion for the need to use the funding for social programs convinced both the majority of the students and the instructor that Congress should use tax money for human welfare and not research on the International Space Station in which there were no guarantees of success. Wasn't the care of a single human life much more important than all the specialized space research in the world?

When the final bell rang, the instructor handed evaluation sheets to each member of the debate team. Sarah beamed as she saw an "A" at the top of the page. Her hard work had paid off once again. Walking down the hallway she scanned the points she received in each of the categories on the teacher's rubric. All of them were either the maximum number of points or one point away.

"Great job," Ryder said as he matched strides with her. "You almost had me convinced, but I didn't want to change positions midstream and get marked down for it."

Sarah looked up and laughed. "Thanks," she replied. "You weren't so bad yourself."

A blast of cold air greeted the pair as Ryder opened the door for Sarah. Both instinctively pulled their coats tightly around their necks. "To celebrate your hard-earned 'A,' how would you like to join me at the Black Angus for an early dinner and then catch a movie at The Capri?"

Sarah's mind raced. *Should I accept his offer for dinner? . . . I decided a long while ago that I'd never have a serious relationship with anyone. . .but a casual dinner with Ryder couldn't possibly lead to anything. . . . Anyway, at this point, who knows if I'll be able to stay in Rocky Bluff much longer. The situation with Mrs. Hatfield could fall through, so I might as well enjoy it.*

"Penny for your thoughts," Ryder teased in order to break the tension her silence was building between them. "Don't look so perplexed. I'm not inviting you to travel on the space station with me."

Sarah turned her attention back to the young man beside her. "Sure, it sounds like fun. After all the time spent working on the project, I need to get out of the dormitory and the library for a while."

"Great! What time would be best for you?" Ryder asked. "Will you be going to the Little Lambs Center later this afternoon?"

"I usually go between four and five every afternoon," Sarah replied. "The only times I've missed have been when I've been sick."

"How about if I pick you up there so you don't have to take the shuttle back to the campus?" Ryder suggested.

Although she was a little shaken by the thought that Ryder might learn the details of her secret, Sarah relaxed and replied, "I'd appreciate the ride. The shuttle is often extremely cold this time of year."

After Ryder nodded and smiled with agreement, Sarah returned their conversation back to their political science class as they walked toward her dormitory. She had gained a small degree of confidence in taking a partial step toward disclosing her long-held secret, but her class work was a much more comfortable topic for her. When they arrived at the entrance of the women's dorm, they said a quick good-bye, and from behind the glass doorway Sarah watched Ryder jog to the parking lot.

Back in her room, Sarah tried to recall everything she knew about Ryder. Other than the fact that he was a good student, well liked by both faculty and students, president of the college's Native Americans' Club and attended church regularly, she realized how little she actually knew about him.

Since the birth of her child, Sarah had not dated anyone. She cringed at the thought of being alone with a man for more than a few isolated moments. *No,* she told herself. *This is not a date. It's merely dinner with a classmate. It won't be any different from having dinner with one of the girls in the dorm.*

❧

Promptly at four o'clock, Sarah rang the doorbell at the Little Lambs Children's Center. Nancy, one of the day workers, answered the door. "Hello, Sarah," she greeted. "Do come in. Charity just got up from her nap and is in the playroom. She's been asking for you."

Sarah hung her coat on a hook by the door and hurried to the playroom. She spotted her daughter lying on the mat playing with Raggedy Ann. "Hi, Mommy," Charity squealed as she held out her arms.

Sarah knelt and picked up her daughter. Holding her close, she kissed her on the forehead. "Hello, Sweetheart. How are you today?"

"I fine," Charity replied, displaying her new set of baby teeth.

Sarah beamed as she carried her daughter to a nearby rocking chair. Each day Charity was adding several new words and short sentences to her vocabulary. Never missing a chance to help increase her daughter's vocabulary, Sarah pointed to the different parts of her body and encouraged her to call them by name.

Within minutes, Dawn entered the playroom and took the rocking chair next to Sarah. The director of the center was rarely seen without one child or another in her arms. "Hi, how's it going?" she greeted.

"Great," Sarah replied. "I'm amazed at how fast Charity's learning to talk. She even knows her colors and the parts of her body."

"Everyone's delighted with her development," Dawn assured her. "Her first wheelchair should be here within a few days and then you'll see a big change in her as she gains control of more and more of her environment."

"I was hoping to be able to take care of Charity by myself as soon as I finished my education and had a good job, but since there's been such a cutback in my financial aid, it looks like my full custody will be delayed," Sarah noted, unable to mask her discouragement.

Dawn did not want to mention that she had spoken with her brother, Jay Harkness, the day before and that several people were working on the possibility of Sarah's assisting Rebecca Hatfield in exchange for her room and board. "I'm sure something will turn up between now and the first of the year. I don't want you to give up hope so easily."

Sarah tried to mask her pessimism. *I've been disappointed so many times before, that I don't want to get my hopes up and then be hurt again.*

Dawn quickly changed the subject. "Jeff Blair called this afternoon to check on Charity," she explained brightly. "He sounded very upbeat. He plans to come to Rocky Bluff during Thanksgiving break to spend some time with her."

Sarah smiled. Even though their lives had gone in different directions, she was pleased that Jeff was taking an active interest in his daughter's life. She and Jeff had become intimate during one reckless summer while they were in high school. Jeff had been in Billings for a high school football camp and she had become attracted to him and had let her guard down. When she could no longer hide the possibility that she was pregnant, Sarah made an appointment to see an obstetrician.

After having an ultrasound during her fifth month, Sarah learned that she was not only pregnant, but that her child had spina bifida. At that moment, her life began to collapse. Her mother had insisted that she have an abortion and would have nothing to do with her until she did. Fortunately, Dawn Harkness, the obstetrician's nurse, provided a home for her until the baby was born. A sense of guilt had enveloped the pregnant teen as she tried to bear total responsibility for the unwanted pregnancy. However, under a strange set of circumstances, when the network of Rocky Bluff lovers shared their mutual joys and concerns, Jeff learned Sarah's secret. Refusing to let her carry the total responsibility for their mistake, Jeff stepped forward and helped with the financial support of little Charity.

"Great, I'm glad he can come," Sarah replied to Dawn after a moment of reflection. "I'd like to see him again myself and fill him in on Charity's latest accomplishments. . . .

I wonder if he'll want to see me again. It's been such a long time since we've been together, since I've been in Billings during college breaks the last few times he's been in Rocky Bluff."

The child in Dawn's arms began to fuss, so the director diverted her attention from Sarah and began to speak softly to the baby and pat her on the back. When the little girl finally quit crying, Dawn continued, "Jeff asked if you'd still be in town the week over Thanksgiving vacation. The only time he's able to come is during college breaks and that's usually when you're also on break and go to Billings to see your family. I gave him your number in the dormitory, and he said he'd give you a call before he came."

"Thanks," Sarah replied, her voice barely above a whisper. "Although our lives have gone in different directions, there will always be a bond between us. . .namely little Charity."

Sarah continued playing with her daughter, but in her mind, she began to compare Jeff with Ryder. Of course, their outward appearance was extremely different, but she was now more concerned with inner beauty and character. She had watched Jeff mature from a self-centered high school jock into a compassionate, caring Christian college student. She knew what had made Jeff what he was today, but she had no clue about Ryder's background.

Suddenly Sarah's thoughts were interrupted with the request, "Floor. . .floor."

She smiled at her daughter. "Charity, do you want to play on the mat?"

"Yes," the child replied as she leaned forward in her mother's arms grinning from ear to ear. Even though Charity was not able to move about like normal children her age she was extremely adept at letting everyone know where she wanted to go and what she wanted to do.

Sarah laid her daughter on her stomach on the mat, then went to the toy box and found a small foam ball. Sitting five feet from her, Sarah rolled the ball.

Charity grabbed the ball and smiled proudly. "Catch," she squealed as she threw it in the general direction of her mother. This game continued for several minutes until Ryan Reynolds, the codirector of the center and Dawn's husband, appeared. "Sarah, there's a young man at the door asking for you."

Sarah glanced at her watch and blushed. "We were having so much fun, I forgot the time." She leaned over and gave her daughter a hug and kiss. "Bye, Bye. Mommy's got to go now," she said. "I'll come see you tomorrow."

"I'll finish the game," Ryan laughed as he knelt on the mat and reached for the foam ball. "It will be much easier for you to make an exit without her tears if I distract her."

"Thanks, Ryan," Sarah replied as she hurried from the playroom. "I appreciate it."

Sarah grabbed her coat from the hooks in the lounge, slipped her arms through the sleeves and stepped into the late November air where Ryder was waiting.

"Hi," she greeted brightly. "I'm sorry to keep you waiting."

Ryder took her arm and escorted her to his car. "I didn't think you saw me pull up, so I thought I'd better ring the bell. I hope you didn't mind."

"I should have been watching for you, but I got so involved with what I was doing that I forgot the time," Sarah explained as she slid into the passenger seat of his green sports car.

Ryder closed the door behind her and then hurried around and slipped behind the wheel. "I admire your dedication in volunteering to help with the disabled children, especially when you don't have any personal connection with any of them."

Sarah gulped. She felt she had to be honest, but she had never before shared her secret with any of her college classmates. A multitude of questions flashed before her. *What will his reaction be? Will he ever want to see me again? Could he also have a hidden secret in his background?*

Lights began to brighten the streets as dusk settled over the community of Rocky Bluff, Montana. For the next few blocks, they drove in silence enjoying the fading sunset. Finally, Sarah developed enough courage to break the silence. "To tell you the truth," Sarah began. "I have a personal interest at Little Lambs. I'll explain it over dinner."

Ryder's dark eyes sparkled as he surveyed the attractive passenger beside him through his rearview mirror. "I thought there had to be more to the story than what met the eye," he replied, "and I'm looking forward to hearing all about it. In the meantime. . .was that Ryan Reynolds that answered the door?"

"Yes, it was," Sarah replied, thankful for the change in subjects. "Did he recognize you?"

Ryder shook his head. "Oh no, I was just a little kid when he was in high school. In fact, if his name hadn't been on the plaque outside, I probably wouldn't have recognized him at all."

"Ryan does most of the administrative work, plus maintains the building and also helps with the children whenever needed. He's so good with them and they all love him," Sarah explained. "It wouldn't surprise me if Dawn and Ryan would be starting a family of their own soon."

Ryder turned into the parking lot of the Black Angus Steak House, parked his car, and then escorted Sarah into the restaurant. As if sensing their need for privacy, a friendly hostess led them to a back booth. Within minutes, a waitress brought them two glasses of iced water and took their order.

While they were waiting for their food, Ryder looked sympathetically into Sarah's deep hazel eyes. "Would you like to share what your personal interest is in Little Lambs now? I can tell it means an awful lot to you."

Sarah took a deep breath. She knew that sooner or later she would have to tell her story, so it might as well be now. Besides, what difference would it make, she wasn't even sure she'd be in Rocky Bluff after semester break. "I haven't even told this to my roommate, Vanessa," she began hesitantly as she studied Ryder's face for any expression of rejection. "The reason I spend so much time at Little Lambs Children's Center is that one of the children in the home is my own."

Ryder's eyes widened and his face flushed. "I'm sorry. I didn't mean to pry into your personal life."

"That's okay," Sarah assured him. "I feel I can trust you. I made a very stupid mistake when I was in high school. Even though I know God has forgiven me, many people have suffered because of it, especially little Charity."

Ryder paused a moment for Sarah to collect her thoughts. "Since she's at Little Lambs does that mean she's disabled?"

"I'm afraid so," she explained. "She was born with a severe case of spina bifida and hydrocephalus. Some people encouraged me to have an abortion, but I just couldn't go through with it. . . . Every time I see how sweetly Charity is developing, I'm so glad that I didn't. She is the most precious thing in the world to me."

"I'm glad you didn't give in to the pressure," Ryder assured her. "I've never understood how people could use abortion as a form of birth control."

Sarah shook her head. "If Dawn hadn't come into my life at that time, I don't know what I would have done. She provided both physical and emotional support during a very difficult time. When she and Ryan married and started Little

Lambs, Charity was their first resident. I've been going to the center every day not only to spend time with my daughter, but also to learn how to care for disabled children. As soon as I finish school and get a good-paying job, I want to raise her myself," Sarah explained. That's why I was so upset when I didn't get enough financial assistance to finish my associate's degree this spring."

"I'm sure something will work out for you," Ryder tried to assure her. Then, as if sensing she had shared as much as she was comfortable with at that time, he changed the subject, "I'm extremely fortunate that all my college expenses are paid by a grant from my Indian reservation. Sometimes I feel a little guilty when I see how other students have to work plus take out huge student loans just to get through college while I have all my expenses paid."

"You're extremely fortunate," Sarah noted as the waitress served their plates of filet mignon. "What are you majoring in?"

"I'm taking basic general education classes here at Rocky Bluff, but I plan to transfer to the University of Iowa and enroll in their Physician's Assistant program. I heard they have one of the best in the country. When I complete my education, I plan to return to the reservation where my grandparents live and help my own people. They have a fantastic medical clinic at the reservation near Running Butte, but it seems that they're always short of medical services. Dawn Reynolds's aunt founded the clinic nearly twenty years ago."

"I've heard of Running Butte, but I don't know too much about it," Sarah replied with interest. "I think Ryan Reynolds also has a brother that lives there."

"You're getting to know the local history well," Ryder laughed.

"His brother Larry runs Harkness Hardware Two, and his wife, Libby, is a paralegal for the tribal attorney. I see him in the store almost every time I go back. They're a real nice family and have done a lot to help improve the standard of living for those on the reservation."

The young couple enjoyed a few bites of their filets, baked potatoes, and vegetables in silence. Both relaxed in the openness of their conversation. As their eyes accidentally met, they both smiled. "This is excellent," Sarah exclaimed. "I'm afraid I'm going to put on five pounds from this meal alone."

"If you do, you'll burn it off tomorrow, as hardworking as you are," Ryder teased.

Sarah blushed and responded with a grin. Ryder continued, "If I remember right, Larry Reynolds went through some pretty difficult years while he was in his late teens. I don't know all the details, but the Harknesses were instrumental in helping him get straightened out. I think they also named one of their children Charity."

"That's interesting," Sarah replied. "I picked the name Charity because she was a source of so much love. Because of her, I learned the love of my family, friends, a church community, and most importantly, I learned about the love Jesus Christ had for me."

Ryder reached for Sarah's hand. "That's such an inspiring story. You shouldn't be ashamed of what you've been through. You should use it to encourage high school kids about the dangers of what can happen through careless decisions. They need to be reminded whatever problems they may face, Jesus is sufficient to meet their needs."

Sarah paused, glad to hear his words of faith and also challenged by them. Her eyes settled on a distant mural. "I never thought of it in those terms. . . . Maybe I shouldn't hide the lessons I've learned the hard way, but instead turn the painful situation into a teaching tool. I'll have to give it some thought and prayer."

Ryder and Sarah finished their meal, paid the cashier, and drove to the Capri Theater where a two-year-old comedy was playing. They realized they could rent similar movies at the video rental store, but nothing could compare to the wide screen, the smell of popcorn, and being surrounded by friends and neighbors.

The evening ended all too soon. As Ryder walked Sarah to the front entrance of her dormitory he asked, "When you were in Sunday school as a child did you ever learn the song, 'This Little Light of Mine, I'm Going to Let It Shine'?"

Sarah had only attended Sunday school a few times as a child, but when she was there, that had been her favorite song. "Are you trying to tell me that I'm hiding my light under a bushel basket?" she replied lightheartedly as the truth of the words seared deeply into her soul.

Ryder put his arm around her and pulled her close. "What do you think?" he asked seriously.

four

Large flakes of snow slowly drifted to the ground as Sarah strolled across the campus of Rocky Bluff Community College the week before Thanksgiving. The beauty of the first snowfall of the season escaped her as her mind bounced from her fear that she would have to return to Billings at the end of the semester to look for a job to her sense of relief at still being accepted by a classmate after sharing her secret about Charity. Suddenly her thoughts returned to her surroundings as a voice behind her shouted, "Sarah, wait up."

Sarah turned. "Hi, Ryder," she greeted as his tall dark form ran to catch up with her. "I missed you in political science class today."

"I had a flat tire on the way to school and by the time I got it changed, the class was over," Ryder said. "When I explained the situation to our instructor she was kind enough to give me the notes of her lecture, but I wish I'd been a part of the class discussion. I always enjoy a good heated debate."

Sarah giggled as the two slowly walked toward her dormitory. "It was rather boring today," she confided. "Josh got on his liberal soapbox again and no one else got a chance to say much. Fortunately, after a few minutes of his monologue, the instructor redirected the conversation. We began discussing the fallacy of the Iowa Straw Poll and how Iowa has caucuses instead of primaries during each presidential election year."

"How boring," Ryder said with mock disgust. "I'm glad I wasn't there." He then glanced at his watch. "It's almost four. Are you planning to go to Little Lambs this afternoon?"

"I wouldn't miss it for anything," Sarah assured him. "I wanted to drop my books off in my room and then head for the shuttle stop."

"Would you like a ride? I'm going right by there."

Sarah smiled, pleasantly surprised that Ryder seemed more interested in her than ever. "Sure, it's a lot better than sitting on the bench collecting snow," she chuckled. "Would you mind waiting in the lobby? I'll hurry to my room, leave my books, and get the toy I just bought for Charity."

❧

Ryder Long stood at the window of the women's dormitory lobby while Sarah hurried down the hallway to her room. Since he was hoping to someday become a physician's assistant and possibly specialize in pediatrics, his interest in the Little Lambs Children's Home intensified. A fresh idea flashed through his mind. He loved working with children and seeing their excited smiles when he had brought momentary joy into their lives. Also, knowing the competition in the medical field, he was always interested in projects that would give him practical experience with children and would add strength to his résumé. *I wonder if they use volunteers at Little Lambs to help with the children. I wonder how I can become involved without appearing like I'm only doing it to impress Sarah.*

Hearing footsteps behind him, Ryder turned and watched Sarah hurrying down the hall toward him; her purse was slung over her left shoulder while she grasped a small sack in her right hand. Her bright smile always lifted his spirits. "Ready?" he asked as she approached.

"Sure am," Sarah replied as Ryder held the door open for her. "The older Charity gets the stronger the bond is becoming between us. I can hardly wait until I'm able to care for her myself."

Ryder took Sarah's hand as they walked toward the parking

lot. The snow was getting heavier with each passing minute. "You've talked so much about Charity since you first told me about her, that I'd love to meet her. Do you think that might be possible sometime?"

Sarah beamed. "How about today? She's learning how to talk and it's so much fun hearing her try to use the new words she's learned."

When the pair arrived at Little Lambs, they found Charity playing in the ball pit. She loved lying in the pile of balls and throwing them in all directions. "Mommy," she squealed, holding her arms out to be picked up, as Sarah and Ryder entered the playroom.

Sarah picked up her daughter and carried her to the sofa with Ryder following closely behind. "How are you today?" Sarah asked, giving her daughter a big hug.

"I fine," Charity replied with a grin.

"This is Ryder," Sarah said as she motioned to her friend beside her. "Can you say 'Hi' to Ryder?"

"Hi, Ryder," Charity cooed as he reached out to squeeze her hand. Instead, Charity raised her chubby arms toward him. "Hold, hold."

Sarah and Ryder exchanged pleased glances as she handed her daughter to his waiting arms.

Charity grinned at him and began to rub his cheeks. "Pretty, pretty," she cooed. Her infectious warmth immediately won Ryder's heart as he began to play finger games and sound games with her. An hour and a half passed before they realized the time.

"I'd better get out of here before I miss the last shuttle of the evening," Sarah gasped as she glanced at her watch.

"Don't worry about it," Ryder assured her. "I'll give you a ride back to the campus."

At last, the pair said good-bye to little Charity and handed her to Dawn Reynolds who had just entered the playroom to start preparing the children for the evening meal. Sarah's heart nearly broke as she heard Charity cry out, "Mommy, no go. Mommy, no go."

Knowing what had to be done, Sarah blew her daughter a kiss from across the room, put on her coat, and stepped into the early darkness. About two inches of snow had accumulated while they were inside. Ryder opened the passenger door for her, walked around the car, slid behind the wheel, and started the engine. He then took his snow scraper from under his seat and began sweeping the snow from the car.

As Ryder worked, Sarah watched with fondness. Here was a man who was strong and masculine, and yet exhibited such gentleness while playing with Charity and the other children. *With his charisma with small children, he'll be excellent working in pediatrics,* she thought. *In spite of being extremely intense and serious, Ryder has a mysterious inner spark that seems to calm the children while it brings excitement into their play.*

When the engine was warm and they were on their way, Ryder turned south toward the college. They rode in silence for a few moments before he spoke. "Sarah, I feel sorry for you and Charity and all those other precious children. It just doesn't seem fair that some are born with such terrible birth defects. I'd like to do whatever I possibly can to help."

Sarah flushed with frustration. "I'm not interested in people's sympathy and neither are the children," she protested. "Those children are like any others, except they need a little more understanding and assistance because of their disabilities."

Now it was Ryder's turn to turn red. "I. . .I know," he stammered, "but I can't help but feel sorry for them. Their twisted bodies are so pathetic, it just makes my heart ache to see them."

Sarah rode in silence the remainder of the way to the campus. *Just when I thought that I'd found a friend who would understand me and my intense love for Charity, but I'm disappointed again,* she thought. *Ryder is too wrapped up with the disability to see the intensity of the human spirit within.*

Upon arriving at the campus, Sarah gave a polite "thank you" and hurried in to her dormitory, hoping to clear her frustrations about being the object of pity instead of understanding. Upon opening her door, she spotted a note in her roommate's familiar scrawled handwriting taped onto her telephone. "Call Teresa Olson" with a phone number.

I wonder why our minister's wife would be calling me, she asked herself as she removed her coat and hung it in the closet. Sarah picked up the phone and punched the appropriate buttons. "Hello, this is Mrs. Olson," a gentle voice answered the ringing telephone.

"This is Sarah Brown. I just returned from Little Lambs and found a note to call you."

"Hello, Sarah," Teresa replied. "How have you been doing? You generally leave church so early that I rarely get a chance to visit with you."

"I've been pretty busy lately, getting ready for final exams. I have several major papers that are due within two weeks."

"Most college students are swamped this time of year," Teresa acknowledged and then took a deep breath, indicating that she was ready to get to the real purpose of her call.

"I understand that you might be interested in finding a place where you could work for your room and board while you finish your education."

"That's true," Sarah sighed. "I'm only going to be able to receive enough financial aid next semester to pay for my tuition and books, but not enough to pay for my housing and food. I don't want to drop out of school, but so far I don't have any other options."

"If things can be worked out, we may have a solution for you," Teresa continued confidently. "Rebecca Hatfield needs someone to fix her breakfast and evening meal, make sure she takes her medications on time, and stay with her at night. We are arranging for her to have home services with her during the day, but if we can't find anyone to stay with her in the evenings, she'll have to be cared for in a nursing home. We'd like to postpone that as long as possible."

Sarah gasped as her eyes widened. She was willing to try almost anything in order to finish her education and this situation seemed almost tailor made for her. "My advisor, Jay Harkness, told me a little about her problems. I remember her husband's bringing her to church every Sunday, but he always took her home right after the service so I never got to actually meet her."

"She once had a very sweet personality," Teresa explained sadly, "but Alzheimer's disease is taking a real toll on her and she is becoming extremely unpredictable and needs closer supervision. Would you like to go over and meet her and decide if you would want to take the job?"

"Sure," Sarah replied without hesitation. "When would be a good time?"

"How about Saturday afternoon at two thirty?"

"That's fine with me."

"I'll pick you up at the dormitory and take you to Rebecca's house. After meeting with her and looking over the situation, if you're still interested I could take you to see David Wood. He's the attorney who is trustee over her legal and financial care.

"Some of your responsibilities will include getting Rebecca up in the morning, helping her bathe and dress, and making sure she takes her medicine and has a good breakfast," Teresa

Olson explained. "In the evening you'll need to see that she eats supper and later help her prepare for bed. One of the most important things is to watch her for safety issues. She has been known to wander out at night and to leave the burners lit after she was done cooking."

Sarah nodded as she listened intently. The more Teresa talked, the more interested she became in the challenge of helping Rebecca Hatfield.

"Too often young people would not have the patience or understanding to work with Alzheimer's patients," the pastor's wife noted, "but you have a special compassion and understanding for the disabled. I'm certain you'd be a great caregiver for Rebecca."

Sarah remembered her emotions toward Ryder's sympathetic comments less than an hour before. Disabled people need understanding, not sympathy. She was determined not to slip into that mode of thinking herself.

❧

As soon as Sarah finished classes the next afternoon, she hurried to the computer lab where she could have Internet access. She immediately did a search for the Alzheimer Association's web page. She sat with her eyes glued to the screen, following as many links as possible that helped her learn about the disabling disease. Before beginning her research, Sarah was only aware of the short-term memory loss and was not aware of the disturbance in behavior and appearance that could also be observed. She learned that she needed to be prepared to face agitation, irritability, quarrelsomeness, and Rebecca's diminishing ability to dress appropriately.

All night Sarah tossed and turned in her bed. She began to question whether she was up to the challenge. She prayed for wisdom to make the right decisions and strength to face whatever the future would hold. By morning, Sarah was exhausted, but she felt a peace that whatever happened, God was in control of the situation.

At 2:30 the next afternoon, Sarah waited at the front door of the dormitory for Teresa Olson. As soon as she recognized Teresa in her blue van when it pulled to the curb, Sarah hurried to the vehicle.

"Hi, Sarah," the pastor's wife greeted, as she opened the van door and motioned for the coed to join her. "It's good to see you again. When I talked with Rebecca this morning, she was looking forward to meeting you, but don't be surprised if she doesn't remember anything about that conversation this afternoon."

"During the last two days I've done a lot of reading about Alzheimer's," Sarah responded. "I hope this arrangement will work out. Helping Rebecca could be an answer to both our prayers."

Teresa explained more of the responsibilities that caring for a person with Alzheimer's would involve as she drove through the snow-packed streets of Rocky Bluff. When Teresa stopped her vehicle in the Hatfields' driveway, Sarah said, "It's a lovely home. I can understand how one person could become very lonely in such a large home. Maintaining it must be overwhelming to Rebecca."

Both women exchanged glances and smiled as they saw a hand holding back the front curtains and a set of intense gray eyes watching them.

"It looks like Rebecca remembered and could scarcely wait for us to arrive," Teresa laughed.

Rebecca threw open the door before Teresa had a chance to ring the bell. "Mrs. Olson, please come in," she greeted. "I'm glad you could visit me."

"It's good to see you again," Teresa greeted as she gave Rebecca a quick hug. "I'd like you to meet Sarah Brown," she continued as she motioned to Sarah.

Sarah stepped forward and shook the frail woman's hand. "Rebecca, it's nice to meet you. You have such a lovely home."

"Are you the one who's going to live with me?" Rebecca queried.

Sarah smiled. "I hope so."

"Then follow me and I'll show you your bedroom," the older woman said, not wanting to waste any time with formalities. "I hope you'll be able to stay with me, because I don't want to have to go to a nursing home."

Sarah's heart melted as she saw the desperate look in Rebecca's soft eyes. "I'll see what I can do to help you," Sarah promised. "Maybe together we can help each other and solve both our problems."

Rebecca took Sarah's hand as she led her down the hallway. "I've always liked helping other people," she exclaimed, "but lately, I'm having trouble even taking care of myself. The only thing I can do to help you is to offer you a place to stay."

"This is a lovely room," Sarah said as Rebecca proudly opened the door to the bedroom. Sarah's eyes immediately fell on the handmade bedspread. "Did you crochet the bedspread? It's beautiful."

"I did that a long time ago," Rebecca replied proudly. "I don't think I'd be able to do it today. Do you crochet?"

Sarah shook her head. "I've never taken the time, but maybe you could teach me a few basic stitches."

❧

Teresa smiled as she watched a rapport build between the coed and the fragile, older woman. This was exactly what she had wanted to see. In order for the proposed arrangement to work, Sarah's most important task was to gain the love and respect of Rebecca so that she could work with her in such a way as to minimize the older woman's confusion and agitation level.

❧

Before the afternoon was over, Sarah agreed to move into one of Rebecca's spare bedrooms on January 3, the day before classes were to begin following Christmas vacation. Sarah could scarcely contain her relief. "Rebecca seemed so sweet," she said, as Teresa backed the blue van out of the driveway. "Since I didn't know her well before, it was hard for me to tell that she had any memory problems at all."

"For the short term, Rebecca is often able to mask her disability if she concentrates hard enough," Teresa explained, "but as you spend more time with her, you'll recognize that her recall is still fairly acute, but her problem-solving abilities have become extremely limited. Her judgment in taking care of herself can no longer be trusted. She often forgets her medicines, forgets to turn off a burner on the stove, or fails to bathe or dress herself properly."

Sarah's eyes sparkled and the corners of her mouth continued to rise. "This is truly an answer to my prayers. Besides being able to help Rebecca, I'll be able to stay in college and visit Charity regularly," she exclaimed. "Since you'll be going right by Little Lambs, would you mind dropping me off there? I can hardly wait to tell Dawn Reynolds the good news."

"No problem," Teresa replied. "She and her brother have been working hard trying to find a way for you to be able to stay in school."

Just as Teresa had predicted, Dawn was overjoyed to learn of the arrangement with Rebecca Hatfield. After listening to Sarah's excited explanation, she, too, had news to share. "Sarah, Jeff Blair called this morning. He's planning on spending Thanksgiving vacation in Rocky Bluff so he can have some time with Charity. He asked if you were planning to stay in town or go to Billings during the break. He sounded as though he wants to spend some time with you as well."

Sarah's eyes brightened even more. "I was thinking about taking the bus to Billings for Thanksgiving, but I haven't seen Jeff since last summer. I could easily be persuaded to stay in the dormitory."

"I don't mean to pry," Dawn said cautiously, "but I was wondering about your relationship with Ryder. I was getting the impression something serious was developing between the two of you."

Sarah shook her head. "I don't think I'm going to continue seeing him," she replied. "He's a nice guy and everything, but ever since he learned about little Charity I feel that he looks on us as objects of pity. I told him that I wanted understanding instead of sympathy."

"I appreciate how you feel," Dawn replied, "but some people have trouble expressing the difference between sympathy and empathy." The former nurse paused while she comforted the fussing child in her arms before continuing. "Ryder seems to be developing quite an interest in disabled children. He stopped by early this morning and signed up on our volunteer list."

Sarah's eyes widened. "Really? When is he going to help?"

"We have trouble getting volunteers on Sunday afternoons because most people want to be with their families," Dawn replied, "but since he's single he's more than willing to spend Sundays with the children."

Sarah looked down, her face flushed. "That was thoughtful of him," she replied softly. "Maybe I did misread his intentions and jumped to the wrong conclusion."

Dawn put her hand on Sarah's shoulder. "Don't blame yourself," she said. "There's nothing to prevent you from still being friends without having a romantic involvement."

Sarah hung her head. "I think I owe Ryder an apology for being so short with him about not wanting his sympathy. However, I would also like to spend time with Jeff while he's here." Sarah paused and then her silence turned to laughter. "I've spent nearly three years thinking I'd never have a date again in my life and now I'm having a chance to possibly see two different guys."

"The Lord works in mysterious ways," Dawn reminded her. "I think it's time you accept your past, and see yourself as an attractive young woman who possesses a wealth of gifts and talents to offer to the world. Just because you made a mistake when you were sixteen years old doesn't mean you are branded for life. You have asked God for forgiveness, and He has forgiven you. Now it's time for you to forgive yourself and go on with your life."

five

"Lord, on this Thanksgiving Day we'd like to thank You for this bountiful feast and for all the many blessings You have provided for us," Ryan Reynolds prayed. He lifted his eyes and glanced around the table at the toddlers in their specially designed highchairs and the parents who sat beside them. His heart became overwhelmed with gratitude. "Thank You, God, for these precious children whom You have given us the privilege of caring for and for their parents who have loved them through the difficult moments along with the good times. May we continue to walk in Your love and mercy throughout our remaining days on earth. In Jesus' name, Amen."

Four long tables laden with all types of festive foods had been pushed together in the playroom of Little Lambs Children's Center. All but two of the children had family members to help celebrate Thanksgiving together. Dawn Reynolds's mother, Nancy Harkness, had worked for two weeks preparing food for the first annual Little Lambs Family Thanksgiving Dinner. The children giggled with delight at the extra attention they were receiving. Dawn and Ryan basked in the interest the parents were showing their children, and Nancy Harkness enjoyed the opportunity to be of service to such an important ministry.

Little Charity Blair sat in a form-fitted highchair between Sarah Brown and Jeff Blair. As the turkey, dressing, and all the side dishes were passed, Sarah prepared a small plate for Charity before she filled her own plate. She was careful to either mash the food or cut it into extremely small pieces.

Sarah helped Charity guide the spoon toward her mouth and ignored it when the three-year-old used her fingers instead. Jeff watched Charity try to feed herself, and then compared her with the children of similar age. Although the others were messy and alternated between using their fingers and a spoon or fork, they ate independently. Jeff leaned behind Charity's chair and whispered to Sarah, "I thought Charity had average intelligence. Why isn't she able to feed herself like the others?"

"She is normal," Sarah smiled, "but she is what they call 'orally defensive.' She has trouble accepting different textures and tastes in food. Even brushing her teeth can sometimes be a real nightmare."

Jeff's face flushed. "I didn't know that," he whispered. "I wish I could spend more time with her and learn more about the various challenges she faces."

"I know you're doing the best you can," Sarah tried to assure him. "Charity is getting the best care possible, but right now it's important that you and I complete our education, and find good jobs so that we can take on more responsibility for her care."

Jeff nodded in agreement and turned his attention back to the turkey drumstick on his plate. "I have a year and a half before I complete my degree in physical education. When I finish, I hope there will be a job for me close to Rocky Bluff. I never realized how much being a father would mean to me when she was first born. I have to admit, the older I get the more Charity tugs on my heartstrings."

The day passed swiftly for the happy gathering. At two o'clock, the children were taken to the sleeping rooms and put down for their afternoon naps. While they slept, the parents gathered in the playroom. They all helped clear the table. While the women loaded the dishwasher and straightened the kitchen, the men took down the folding tables and rearranged the chairs.

After the work was completed, Dawn motioned for everyone to place their chairs in a circle and said, "We all come from a variety of backgrounds, but we share a common interest—the love of a child with spina bifida. Most of us have read a great deal about the disability but feel isolated in the personal struggles that we face trying to do what's best for our child. Now might be a good time to share the joys, challenges, and heartaches you've faced as parents of children with disabilities."

Everyone nodded with agreement and looked nervously around the room to see who would have the courage to speak first. Much to Sarah's surprise, Jeff began sharing his feelings of guilt concerning the pregnancy and the child's disability and the decisions he faced as a single father trying to do what was right for his daughter and her mother, and most importantly, before God.

Jeff's honest confession helped others obtain the courage to share many of their deepest fears concerning their child. They no longer felt isolated in their struggles. A bond of friendship developed among them and they soon were exchanging addresses, telephone numbers, and e-mail addresses.

When the little ones began waking, they were brought out to the families in the playroom. The activities shifted from being adult-centered to child-centered as, one by one, the parents started playing with their own child. When Charity awoke, Jeff and Sarah sat on the floor and stacked blocks with her until they toppled to the floor. Each time they fell, Charity would laugh with an infectious giggle that caused the others to follow suit. Before they realized it, the sun had set and it was time to feed the children a light evening meal, have an hour of quiet, and put them to bed.

After the children were in their beds, the parents bade each other farewell and promised to try to get together at Christmastime. As Jeff and Sarah stepped into the crisp late fall air, they looked at each other, unable to say good-bye after a nearly perfect day. "How about taking in the late show at the theater tonight?" Jeff asked. "When I drove through town this morning I noticed there's a good comedy playing tonight at the Capri. Would you be interested in seeing it with me?"

"Sounds like fun," Sarah replied as her heart began to race and her face flushed.

Jeff instinctively took her arm and led Sarah to the car on the pretext of keeping her from slipping on the ice. But a new sense of warmth and protection spread over him. He had dated several different girls at the University of Montana. Although they were exciting and nice looking, he never felt so comfortable with any other girl as he did at that moment with Sarah. As they shared laughs throughout the movie, Jeff was sure he wanted to see more of the mother of his child, but he, like Sarah, was committed to completing his education above all else.

When the movie was over, the pair stood to leave. As they waited for the lines to clear Sarah gasped, "I've never laughed so much in my life. If there wasn't a funny line on the screen, you were whispering something hilarious in my ear."

"They say laughter is the best medicine," Jeff replied lightly and hesitated briefly before continuing. "And from what I've seen you've been working much too hard and haven't taken enough time to just relax and enjoy life."

Sarah squeezed Jeff's hand as the line began to move. "You have excellent insight into my mind and soul. I feel better tonight than I have in a long time."

The pair exchanged puns, jokes, and silly stories as they drove across town. When they arrived at the parking lot, Jeff escorted Sarah to her dormitory. "It's been a memorable day," he said as he took her hand in his. "I'd like to spend as much time as possible with both you and Charity while I'm in Rocky Bluff. What do you think of the idea of taking her to the mall tomorrow to look at the Christmas decorations? She seems fascinated by bright, flashing lights. I'm not comfortable having total care of her, but you seem to be ready to step in as full-time caregiver."

"I wish that were true," Sarah sighed, "but I still have a lot to learn." She hesitated. She had longed for a chance to do more things with her daughter, but without a car of her own, she had been unable to even consider it. It would be nice to have their daughter to themselves. "We could talk to Dawn about taking Charity to the mall. The malls are crowded the day after Thanksgiving, but we could go early in the day and avoid the rush."

"Why don't I pick you up at nine thirty and we can go to Little Lambs together," Jeff suggested. "If we can't take Charity out, then we could stay there and play with her. If you'd agree, I'd take you to lunch during her nap time."

"Sounds good to me," Sarah replied and then tried to muffle a yawn. "I'm looking forward to tomorrow, but right now I think it's time to get some shuteye."

That night Sarah tossed in her bed. Images of the laughter she had had throughout the day with Jeff kept bouncing against the serious concern and compassion she felt when she was with Ryder. In many ways, they were alike. Both men were strong Christians who attended church regularly. They both loved their families and took their education seriously. However, in other ways they were very different from each other. Ryder was quieter and more serious around people, while Jeff was outgoing and gregarious. Ryder immediately struck a rapport with the children with disabilities, while

Jeff appeared to be a little awkward with the other children at Little Lambs.

It's ironic, Sarah thought, *for more than three years I refused to be attracted to men, but now I find myself attracted to two at the same time.*

Sarah's roommate, Vanessa White, had gone home for the holidays, so Sarah enjoyed the luxury of sleeping later in the morning without interruption. At nine o'clock, the loud ringing of her telephone awakened her. Sarah stumbled to the desk under the window. "Hello," she murmured.

"Hello, Sarah. Did I awaken you?" a familiar voice asked as the coed slumped into the chair at the desk.

"Oh, hi, Mom," Sarah replied as she stretched and became more alert. "I guess I did oversleep a little this morning."

"You probably needed the rest," Doris Brown replied in her soft motherly tone. "I'm sure you've been spending too much time hovering over books and computers and not getting enough sleep."

"I have been doing a lot of studying lately," Sarah admitted, "but I think my immediate problem was that I stayed out too late last night with Jeff Blair."

"So Jeff's in Rocky Bluff for the Thanksgiving holidays?" her mother teased. "I wondered why you postponed your visit home."

The mother-daughter relationship between Sarah and Doris had not always been this close. Four years ago, upon learning that her daughter was pregnant, Doris had insisted that she get an abortion, and when Sarah refused, Doris disowned her during the most difficult time in her life.

Yet through that troubled time, Sarah learned about the love and forgiveness of Jesus Christ. Doris Brown was so moved by the change in her daughter and the birth of her first grandchild that she reconciled and accepted the same

Christian love and forgiveness that Sarah had embraced. From that time forward, the family warmth and understanding far exceeded what either one ever thought possible.

"Mother, don't get the wrong idea," Sarah responded lightly. "I stayed behind because I was out of money and couldn't afford a bus ticket. I really wanted to see you and Mark."

Doris shook her head. "Why didn't you tell me? I would have sent money for a ticket," she scolded.

"Mom, you work hard for what you have and don't have that much to spare," Sarah protested with a lump building in her throat, "and besides, I want to be able to make it on my own."

Doris smiled to herself as she recalled the stubborn self-reliance that had always seemed a part of her daughter's personality, even before she became pregnant with Charity. "I'm very proud of all you've accomplished," she assured her daughter, "but your brother and I would both like to see you. Besides, he's taking driver's education and needs to get some practice time on the road. We were wondering if it would be okay if we came to Rocky Bluff Sunday to see you and Charity?"

Sarah's eyes brightened. "Of course it's okay. I'd love to have you come," she exclaimed. "I have some good news for you, but I'll wait until you get here to tell you."

Doris Brown snickered with affection for her daughter. "You know how I hate secrets. Do I have to wait two days before I find out?"

"I'm afraid you'll have to because I'm good at keeping secrets," Sarah teased. "I'm looking forward to seeing you. What time do you expect to arrive?"

Doris hesitated while she did some mental calculations. "If we get an early start we should be there by ten o'clock and then we can go to church with you before we see little Charity. From the last pictures you sent, it looks like she's really grown."

"You won't believe it when you see her," Sarah announced proudly. "She's learning to talk and is becoming extremely expressive. She loves being around people."

"I can hardly wait. I'll be at your dorm around ten Sunday. We can go to brunch after church and then to see Charity."

"Sounds great to me," Sarah responded excitedly. "Good-bye for now. I love you."

"I love you, too. See you Sunday."

As Sarah showered and dressed, she basked in the blessings of the last few days. She had obtained a job, working for her room and board so she would not have to drop out of college; she had found a friend in Ryder Long who she felt accepted her in spite of her troubled background; Jeff had come to Rocky Bluff to see Charity and ended up spending a lot of time with her; and now, her mother and brother were coming to see her.

Sarah hummed her favorite hymn as she hurriedly slipped into a pair of black slacks and a multicolored sweater. She blow-dried her hair and then styled it with her curling iron. She had just finished putting on the final touches of her makeup when she received a call from the receptionist in the dormitory lobby saying that she had a guest waiting for her.

Her face carried an extra glow as she grabbed her coat and hurried to the lobby. Jeff Blair greeted her with a warm hello and a quick hug. "You look happy today. You must have had a good night's rest."

"Just the opposite," Sarah confessed as Jeff opened the door of the dormitory and they stepped into the brisk November air. "I was so wound up from all the laughs we had that I had trouble falling asleep. I didn't wake up until nine o'clock when my mother called."

Through the years, Jeff had developed a special fondness for his baby's grandmother. The last time he had seen Doris

Brown was at Dawn and Ryan Reynolds's wedding two and a half years ago. When Charity was born, Doris had been extremely rude to him, but gradually she was able to forgive him and was able to carry on a pleasant conversation with him at the wedding. "That was nice of her to call. I assume she wanted to wish you a Happy Thanksgiving since you weren't at home yesterday."

"It's even better than that," Sarah exclaimed as they trudged across the frozen parking lot. "She and my brother are coming to Rocky Bluff Sunday. Mark is taking driver's education and needs more practice behind the wheel, so she's going to let him drive the entire way. They're really excited about seeing Charity again."

Jeff opened the car door for Sarah, walked around, and slid behind the wheel. "I'm glad that things are finally working out for your family," he said as he turned the key in the ignition. "Since your mother left her job at the lounge and got one in that fancy restaurant, she seems to be a lot happier."

"She's a totally different woman than she was three years ago," Sarah replied. "She's now the mother that I had always wished that I had."

"There have been so many blessings that came out of Charity's birth," Jeff noted as he reached for her hand while he stopped at a traffic light. "Three years ago the future looked extremely bleak for all of us. . .and now look at it."

Jeff's positive attitude had been one of the main traits that had attracted Sarah to him three years ago. She had always felt overwhelmed with life's problems and Jeff had a special way of helping lift her gloom and making her laugh.

When the pair arrived at Little Lambs, Dawn was pleased that Charity would have a chance to go to the mall with her parents. "The more contact children have with the outside world the better their minds are stimulated," the former nurse explained. "She's already eaten breakfast and you can feed her in the food court when she gets hungry. However, try to get her back before two o'clock. She's used to having a two-hour nap and I'm sure she'll be getting cranky by then."

Sarah and Jeff looked at each other and laughed knowingly. "You can trust us to get her back as soon as she begins to get tired," Sarah replied.

For the next couple of hours, Sarah and Jeff took turns pushing Charity's wheelchair up one side of the mall and down the other. Occasionally, they would let go of the wheelchair and Charity would try to control it herself by pushing on the wheels. Little by little, she gained confidence in her newfound independence. The child's eyes sparkled as she kept saying, "Pretty. . .pretty," whenever bright lights and decorations caught her attention. When they arrived in front of a toy store, Charity tried to turn her wheelchair into the doorway by herself. "Wanna see," she exclaimed as she gave an extra hard push on the wheels.

Jeff and Sarah exchanged glances and laughed. Sarah instinctively took the handles and pushed the chair into the store. They walked slowly up and down the aisle and often stopped to let Charity handle the toys that caught her attention. When she finished looking at each toy, Jeff would return it to its spot on the shelf and go on to another one. When she spotted a miniature chord organ, she reached her arm out. "Wanna see. Wanna see."

Jeff took the little organ from the shelf, turned it on, and set it on Charity's lap. The child laughed with glee as she struck each key one by one. One minute passed, then two, three, and five, while Charity kept experimenting with each of the sounds on the keyboard. "Shall we put the organ back and look at some of the other toys?" Jeff asked as he reached for the organ.

Charity wrapped her arms firmly around the organ. "No. Mine."

Jeff and Sarah could not contain their amusement. "I think we just bought an organ," Jeff chuckled and then turned his attention back to his daughter. "Charity, would you like to buy the organ and take it home with you?"

The little girl grinned. "Want organ."

Jeff reached for an organ that was still in its original container. "Charity, we have to put the organ you have back on the shelf and take this box with the organ to the lady in the front so we can pay for it."

Charity studied the box, making sure that the picture of the organ on the cover was exactly the same as the one in her arms. She reluctantly handed it to her father and reached for the one in his hands. Charity clung tightly to the box while Sarah pushed the wheelchair through the crowded aisles toward the checkout and Jeff followed close behind with an enormous smile on his face. Finally, he was able to give Charity something that he knew she'd really like.

With extra coaxing, Charity released the treasured box long enough for the clerk to scan the bar code, and then Jeff immediately returned it to her waiting arms. As soon as Jeff finished paying for the organ, Charity squealed, "Wanna go home. Wanna go home."

Sarah leaned over the wheelchair. "Don't you want to look in some of the other stores?"

"No," Charity insisted. "Wanna go home now."

The young couple looked at each other, shrugged their shoulders, and said in unison, "I guess that settles that."

Sarah put Charity's coat on her and they headed for the car. Their first outing to the mall was a success, only much shorter than they had hoped.

When they arrived at Little Lambs, Charity insisted on

opening the box as soon as she got inside the door. She kept the organ beside her when she ate a light lunch. At nap time, Charity took it to bed with her. Amused by the intensity of the child's attraction to the organ, Dawn compromised with her and let her take it to bed with her as long as the power was off.

"Looks like we have a budding musician on our hands," Dawn chuckled as she returned to the playroom after putting Charity down for her nap. "Since she'll never be able to walk, music may become a vital outlet for her."

The three continued sharing their experiences with Charity at the mall until there was a loud wail from one of the sleeping rooms and Dawn's responsibility took her to the anxious child.

When they were alone, Jeff turned to Sarah. "While she's sleeping, how about you and I go back to the mall and see the things we didn't get to see when we had Charity? We can make the food court our first stop."

"Sounds great to me," Sarah agreed. The couple said good-bye to Dawn and hurried to the lounge for their coats.

Sarah and Jeff spent the remainder of the afternoon wandering through the variety of stores in the mall. They laughed and joked as if they didn't have a care in the world. When they noticed the lights in the parking lot come on, Jeff said, "Hamburgers are great for lunch, but now it's time for real food. How about dinner at the Black Angus Steak House? I have to leave first thing in the morning to return to Missoula and won't be able to see you or Charity until my next trip."

Sarah readily agreed. This would be a perfect ending for a nearly perfect day. The evening seemed to fly by as the couple laughed and joked together throughout their entire meal. However, in the midst of the gaiety, Sarah couldn't help comparing the evening with the last time she had dinner at the Black Angus with Ryder Long. Both were very special, yet so different. She and Ryder had discussed their pasts, their dreams of the future, and their class work; while she and Jeff knew each other's past, they did not share their class work, but he saw humor and joy in the simplest things of life. Sarah was thankful that they were both simply friends and she would not be forced to choose between the two men.

six

Sarah glanced nervously out her dorm window, anxiously awaiting the arrival of her family. She had not seen her mother and brother since she returned to college after summer vacation. During her summer break, she had worked full-time at the same Pizza Parlor in Billings where she had worked during her high school days. However, this time she was the shift supervisor and found herself overseeing high school students like herself just four years before. During her rare free moments, she marveled at the change in thinking and motivation that had occurred in the high school subculture during the last few years. The young workers displayed a level of disrespect for authority that she would never have imagined when she had been in their position.

Meanwhile the Brown family had the best summer together they had ever had. Her mother had given up her job at the DewDrop several months before and had found a better one as hostess at Milton's Steak House. She no longer wearily fell into bed each night after her shift was over. Plus, she no longer had to count pennies after she paid her rent. Doris Brown was happier than she had been since childhood. Not only was she now attending church regularly, but she had also become active in their women's group and had an entirely new set of friends.

Sarah's brother, Mark, had matured from an awkward adolescent to a vibrant teenager. This past summer he had found a part-time job at the nearby convenience store and was saving his money for his own car. Sarah smiled with amusement as she imagined her mother having to ride all the way to Rocky Bluff with Mark driving so that he could meet his behind-the-wheel requirement for his driver's license.

During the fall, Sarah found her mother's letters and phone calls extremely encouraging. They always seemed to arrive at just the right time when she felt tempted to give up and go home. At the same time, the E-mails from her brother kept her entertained and in touch with what she considered the less serious things of life.

Sarah squinted her eyes as a blue Ford turned into the parking lot. Hoping it was her mother's, she watched as the car parked in the nearly empty lot and a young teen stepped from behind the wheel and a middle-aged woman got out of the passenger seat. Leaving her coat behind, Sarah ran outside into the biting cold to meet her family.

After greeting each with a hug, Sarah led her mother and brother into the holiday-quiet dormitory. Mark glanced around the huge lobby with awe. *So this is how college students live,* he mused. *I wonder if I'll ever be able to go to college. . . . If Sarah can do it, surely I can do it as well.*

Sarah proudly pointed out the TV room, the group study room, the laundry room as they headed down the long hallway toward her room. "This is it," she exclaimed as she threw open the door to her room. "It doesn't always look this way," she laughed. "I spent most of yesterday afternoon cleaning it and my roommate took a lot of her stuff home for Thanksgiving."

"It's very nice, dear," Doris replied as she slowly looked around the small dormitory room. "You've certainly added a homey touch. . .and to think you did it with a lot of ingenuity and little money. I hope you won't have to drop out of school because they cut your financial assistance. You've accomplished so much in the last couple of years."

Sarah beamed, unable to contain her good news. "Mom, I didn't want to tell you until you got here," she exclaimed, "but God answered my prayers in a most unbelievable way. . . . I probably won't have to drop out after all."

"Well, what happened?" Doris urged as she sat on the corner of the bed. "You know I can't stand suspense."

"I think I told you that Dawn's brother is my academic advisor," Sarah began excitedly. "After I explained my situation to him, he talked with our pastor and they were able to arrange for me to work for my room and board for a widow who is in the early stages of Alzheimer's."

"I'm pleased that you're willing to take on such a challenge in order to get your education," Doris said as she put her arm around her daughter. "I just hope it's not too demanding on you."

"I know it's a big step," Sarah replied, "but Rebecca Hatfield is so sweet and I have a lot of support from the church. They don't want her to have to go into a care center until it's absolutely necessary."

Mark began to laugh his typical little-brother chuckle. "What do you know about old people?" he teased.

Sarah returned a phony glare. "I can always learn," she retorted. "I didn't know anything about babies until three years ago, and it won't be long before I'll be able to have permanent custody of Charity."

"We've all learned a lot about basic Christian compassion these last few years," their mother inserted as if trying to alleviate the sibling teasing. "I'm sure you'll be an excellent caregiver for Rebecca." Doris glanced at her watch. "Doesn't your church start at ten thirty?"

Sarah flushed as she hurried to the closet for her coat. "It sure does and it takes a good ten minutes to get there. Mom, do you mind if I drive? I know a few shortcuts."

Mark scowled as Doris handed the car keys to her daughter.

❧

Following church and a Sunday buffet at the Black Angus Steak House, the Brown family hurried to the Little Lambs Children's Center. Doris could scarcely contain her excitement at seeing her granddaughter again. She had brought Sarah to college September 1 and had seen Charity at that time, but she had not seen her since.

"I hope we don't interrupt their nap time," Doris said as Sarah parked the car in front of the Children's Center.

Sarah glanced at the clock on the dash. "They usually start waking up about this time," she replied. "We can wait in the lobby or play with the other children in the playroom until Charity wakes up."

Sarah rang the doorbell to the Children's Center and within seconds, Dawn answered and greeted Doris and Mark with a warm handshake. "I'm glad you could come," she smiled. "Please come in."

"Dawn, it's good to see you again," Doris replied. "How have you been doing?"

"Keeping busy," Dawn laughed, "and you?"

"I guess I can truthfully say exactly the same thing," Doris retorted in jest before she asked seriously, "How has little Charity been doing?"

"Just wonderful." Dawn beamed. "She's becoming quite independent since she's learned to get around by herself in a wheelchair."

Dawn showed Doris and Mark where to hang their coats in the lobby. "Is Charity awake yet?" Doris asked eagerly as she listened for her granddaughter's familiar voice.

"She was one of the first ones to wake up today," the nurse/director replied. "She's with one of the volunteers in the playroom now."

The Browns hurried toward the playroom and then stopped in the doorway when they spotted Charity across the room. She was happily building with blocks on the tray on her wheelchair with a dark-haired young man. They both seemed to be enjoying themselves so much that no one wanted to interrupt their fun. Finally, the young girl looked up. "Mom. . . my," she squealed as she began wheeling herself across the floor toward them.

Instead of rushing toward her daughter, Sarah knelt down with outstretched arms. Charity pushed the wheels as hard as she could to get to her mother. "Wow," Mark gasped. "Look at her go."

As soon as she had gotten across the room, Sarah proudly lifted her from her wheelchair and hugged her. "That was great, Charity," she exclaimed. "You're really getting good with your new set of wheels."

"I'm playing with Ryder," Charity exclaimed as she pointed to the young man who had been building blocks with her.

Ryder strolled across the room and smiled at Sarah. "Hi, Sarah. It's good to see you again. Is this your family?"

Sarah paused as she admired his dark eyes and quiet spirit. "Ryder, I'd like you to meet my mother, Doris Brown, and my brother, Mark."

"Mother, this is Ryder Long. He's in several of my classes and we've worked on several group projects together."

"It's nice to meet you," Doris said as she extended her hand. "Charity seems to be enjoying your company. Do you volunteer here often?"

"I've started coming every Sunday afternoon," Ryder replied as he patted Charity's outstretched hand. "Most of the volunteers need to be with their own families on weekends, and that is the only time that I have free."

"Ryder plans to go on to University of Iowa and become a

physician's assistant," Sarah explained as she continued hugging Charity close to her bosom.

Suddenly a child's voice was heard from the bedroom.

"It sounds like someone else is ready to get up from their nap," Ryder chuckled. "Would you please excuse me?"

As Ryder left the room, all the attention turned to the girl in Sarah's arms. "Hi, Charity," Doris cooed as she reached for her hand. "How are you today?"

"I fine," Charity said in her most grown-up manner.

"I'm your grandma," Doris continued as Charity returned a mildly confused look. "I'm your mommy's mommy."

With those words, Charity began to relax as a smile spread across her face.

"Would you let me hold you?" Doris asked as she stretched out her arms.

Immediately, Charity's smile became broader as she leaned toward her grandmother. Doris took the child with delight and carried her to one of the rocking chairs in the corner. When they were both comfortable, Doris began playing the same finger games she had once played with her own children. When those became tiresome, she pondered the next thing she could do in order to bond with her only granddaughter. Eyeing the books on the shelf beside her, Doris said, "Charity would you like Grandma to read you a story?"

Charity nodded her head. "Story. . .story," she exclaimed excitedly as she pointed to the books beside them.

For the next half hour, Doris and Charity were oblivious to anyone else in the room as they read one story after another. Mark finally became bored and wandered into the lobby where there was a college football game on the television. Not wanting to interrupt her mother's precious moments with her granddaughter, Sarah went to help Ryder get the other children who were beginning to awaken from their naps.

"Your mother seems extremely proud of her granddaughter," Ryder whispered to Sarah as they picked up children in adjoining beds. "It's hard to imagine that she was once so hostile about having a disabled grandchild."

"It's been a miracle beyond my wildest imagination," Sarah replied softly. "Our entire family has completely changed and it's just wonderful. I have so much to be thankful for this Thanksgiving."

Sarah and Ryder continued changing diapers, carrying children to the playroom and getting them interested in various activities. When everyone appeared content, Ryder quietly slipped into the lobby where Mark was engrossed in the football game. "Who's winning?" he asked as he joined the youth on the sofa.

"Texas, right now," Mark replied, "but Oklahoma is getting ready to score again."

The afternoon flew by as the Brown family enjoyed Charity and the other children and Mark found a fellow football enthusiast in Ryder. At five o'clock, the staff began assembling the children into the large dining room for the evening meal. Sarah, her mother, and brother said their farewells and stepped into the brisk late-fall air. Only a faint glow illumined the western sky.

"I hate to see today end," Doris sighed, "but Mark has school tomorrow and we have almost a four-hour drive ahead of us. If you'd like, we could drop you at your dormitory on the way out of town."

"Thanks, Mom," Sarah replied as she gave her a quick hug, "but I think I'll stay and help with supper. Ryder said he'd give me a lift back to campus."

"Hmmm. . .this sounds serious," Mark taunted. "I suppose next thing you're going to tell us is that there are going to be wedding bells."

Sarah returned a teasing scowl. "Mark, he's just a friend. Someday you'll learn that men and women can just be friends without being romantically involved."

"Yeah, sure, Sis," Mark replied as he gave Sarah a good-bye hug. "I'll check with you at Christmastime and see how your love life is going."

Sarah gave her mother a parting hug and then stood in the yard of Little Lambs Children's Center waving as they drove away. Tears filled her eyes. The day had gone so well, it was hard to part, knowing that it would be nearly another month before she would see them again.

Suddenly the trembling coed felt a light hand on her shoulder. "It's sometimes hard to say good-bye, isn't it?" Ryder said softly.

"It sure is," Sarah replied. She brushed away her tear, took a deep breath, and continued, "I suppose I should go in and help Dawn feed the children since she's short of help this weekend."

Ryder nodded with agreement. The pair returned to the kitchen and began washing little fingers as one by one the children finished eating. When she got back to Charity, she noticed her eyes were glazed and she was nonresponsive. Her breathing was labored and her lips were turning blue. Her left arm started convulsing.

"Dawn," Sarah shouted, "what's wrong with her?"

Dawn ran to their side. She made sure Charity did not have any food in her mouth and she peered into the child's eyes. "I don't like the looks of this," she exclaimed as Ryan joined her. "I think we'd better call an ambulance and get her to the hospital."

The next few hours were a blur for the frightened young mother. An ambulance arrived within minutes and quickly whisked Charity away. While Dawn rode in the ambulance with Charity, Ryder and Sarah followed in his green sports car. She whispered a string of prayers under her breath, and Ryder reached for her hand to comfort her. When they arrived at the hospital, Sarah jumped from the car as Ryder stopped the car a few yards from the parked ambulance. She ran behind the gurney into the Emergency Room. Dawn was beside the child, making sure the oxygen mask stayed on her face.

The lab technician drew blood from Charity's arm to run tests, and within minutes, a doctor was talking to the frightened mother. "Sarah, it looks like your daughter had a grand mal seizure. At this time, we don't know what caused it, but it's common for children with neural tube damage to have seizures. I would like to Med-Evacuate her to Great Falls where they can do more testing and she can have a CAT scan. Would you be willing to sign the necessary medical release papers?"

"Of course," Sarah replied mechanically. "Anything to make sure she gets the best care possible." Although a medical team, plus Dawn and Ryder surrounded her, Sarah felt totally alone. None of them could fully understand the fear she felt behind her brave mask. The only one who could possibly share the intensity of her feelings would be the father of her child, and he was many miles away.

While waiting for the medical helicopter to arrive from Great Falls, Sarah slipped out and found a pay phone near the lobby. She reached into her purse and took out an address book. She flipped to the B's and dialed the Missoula number. Her hand trembled while she waited for a response on the other end of the line. Finally, a familiar voice said, "Hello."

"Hello, Jeff," Sarah gasped, almost in tears. "Something awful happened. They think little Charity had a grand mal seizure. They rushed her to the hospital in Rocky Bluff, but the doctor wants to Med-Evac her to the hospital in Great Falls for more testing."

There was a long silence on the other end of the line before there was a response. "What happened? She was so happy Friday when I left," Jeff protested.

"They don't know," Sarah replied, trying to choke back her tears. "It all happened so fast. . . . I'm going to ride with Dawn to Great Falls. We'll probably get there a couple hours behind Charity. The doctor said they'd probably have most of the testing done by the time we get there."

There was a long silence again before Jeff spoke. "I should be at the hospital as well. If I leave right away, I can be in Great Falls in three-and-a-half hours. I'll meet you there."

"Thanks," Sarah replied and then said good-bye, grateful that he was planning to meet them.

When Sarah returned to the Emergency Room, she found Dawn looking for her. "Sarah, we may need to spend the night in Great Falls. Would you like to stop by your dorm room and grab a change of clothes and a toothbrush? I'll need to stop by Little Lambs and get a few things myself. I want to be sure and take a car seat along. I hope we'll be able to bring Charity home with us tomorrow."

The possibility of bringing her daughter home the next day helped ease Sarah's fears. She said a speedy farewell to Ryder and asked him to explain the situation to her instructors and to notify her dorm supervisor that she was called out of town for a family emergency. At this point, she no longer cared about her long-kept secret. Her only concern was for the health and safety of her beautiful daughter.

❧

Sarah was thankful she was with a nurse during the long ride to Great Falls. Dawn was able to explain some of the causes and treatments of seizures and how people learned to live very normal lives in spite of the inconvenience. When they arrived at the hospital, Charity had just finished having the CAT scan and the doctor was waiting for them. A nurse led them into a small conference room where several people were gathered around a long table. "They're meeting concerning Charity's condition," she said as she pushed open the door.

Sarah and Dawn had just introduced themselves and took chairs across from the doctor when the same nurse reappeared in the doorway. "The father is here and would like to be a part of the discussion. Should I show him in?"

Doctor Williams turned to Sarah who smiled and nodded. "By all means," the doctor instructed.

Jeff Blair entered the room. His eyes were heavy and tension lines wrinkled his forehead. The doctor rose, shook the young man's hand, and introduced himself as Doctor Williams. Jeff then greeted Dawn, gave Sarah a hug, and took the chair beside her.

"I'm glad you could all be here," Doctor Williams began in a businesslike fashion. "I know this is an extremely difficult time for you, but fortunately, I have encouraging news for you. The CAT scan did not show any abnormalities, and Charity is now resting normally. We'd like to keep her overnight for observation, but if all goes well, you'll be able to take her home in the morning."

"Thank you," Sarah murmured as she squeezed Jeff's hand.

"What's her prognosis?" Dawn inquired as she studied the doctor's face for any clue. "Will she need medication to control seizures?"

Doctor Williams leaned back in his chair. "At this point there's no way to know," he replied. "She could have another seizure in ten minutes or she may never have another one. I could prescribe medication now, but at the present, I think we'd be better off waiting to see if she has any more seizures before we make a final decision. I'll notify your doctor in Rocky Bluff as to my findings. I'll be making rounds about nine o'clock tomorrow and if all is well I'll dismiss her at that time."

Dawn breathed a heavy sigh of relief. "Thank you very much," she said. "We appreciate all you've done for us."

The doctor shook hands with each of them as he left the conference room. When he was gone, Sarah turned to Dawn. "Do you think it would be possible to see Charity? She looked so terrible the last time I saw her. I need to see her just to alleviate my own fears."

"I'll see what I can do," Dawn replied. "Follow me, and I'll ask the nurse in charge."

Within a few minutes, the three were gathered around the bed where little Charity slept. "She has the face of an angel," Jeff whispered.

"I know," Sarah replied. "She's been through so much in her short lifetime and yet she's always such a happy child."

After everyone was comforted knowing that Charity was all right, the threesome tiptoed from the room. "I'll call and try to get a motel room across the street for us." Dawn said. "Jeff, would you like me to reserve one for you as well? It's been a long day and I'm sure we're all exhausted."

"I'd appreciate that," he replied wearily. "I don't want to leave Great Falls until I'm certain she's going to be all right."

seven

Without taking time for breakfast, Sarah and Dawn showered, dressed, and hurried into the pediatrics ward of the Great Falls hospital. "Good morning, Sleepy Heads," a familiar voice greeted as the two women stepped off the elevator and found themselves face-to-face with Jeff Blair. "Are you going my way?" he teased as he reached for Sarah's hand.

"I think we have a mutual concern just down the hallway," Sarah retorted lightly. "Do you know if she had any further problems last night?"

Jeff's eyes twinkled as he said, "The nurse said that she slept like a baby, so I assume that's a good sign."

"I hope so," Sarah responded seriously, "because I'm looking forward to taking her home this morning."

"I wish I could go back with her," Jeff said with a distant look in his eye, "but I have a couple of term papers due next week and I haven't started my research. I'll need to get back to the university as soon as I know Charity is going to be all right."

As the couple continued discussing their child, Dawn hurried to the nurses' station. "Good morning," she greeted the middle-aged woman studying a patient's chart. "I'm Dawn Reynolds. I currently have custodial care of Charity Blair and was wondering how she is doing."

Without looking up, the nurse responded dryly, "Charity had an unremarkable night with no indication of any further seizures. The doctor will make his rounds before nine o'clock. I assume he will dismiss her today."

"Thank goodness," Sarah injected as she joined Dawn at the counter. "May we see Charity now?"

"Certainly," the ward nurse replied, finally giving the hospital visitors her undivided attention. "The last time I was in there she was awake and playing with toys from the playroom."

The three hurried down the hall to room number 605. Sarah pushed open the door as a broad smile spread across Charity's face. "Mommy," she squealed as she stretched out her arms to be picked up from the crib.

Sarah hugged her daughter, and then Charity made it a game to reach for Dawn and giggled. After Dawn hugged her, Charity reached for Jeff and after a hug from him, she reached for Sarah again. After the three of them had each hugged her four times, they tried to interest her in another game, but were interrupted when the doctor walked into the room followed by the head nurse.

"It looks like she's not lacking in attention," Dr. Williams chuckled.

"Who can resist those baby blue eyes," Jeff replied.

Dr. Williams took the child from her father and laid her on the crib. He did a quick exam and muttered several observations which the nurse quietly recorded on the chart. "She doesn't seem to have any recurring symptoms of the seizure she had yesterday. I'll go ahead and discharge her without prescribing any medication, but if she shows any similar symptoms be sure and get her to the hospital as soon as possible."

"Thank you, so much, for all you've done," Dawn said as the doctor turned to leave. "I'll keep an extra close eye on her for any symptoms that closely resemble another seizure."

The nurse helped them gather the patient's few belongings and then carried Charity down the elevator to the lobby with Dawn, Sarah, and Jeff close behind. "I'll wait here with her, if you'd like to go and get the car," she suggested as Dawn reached into her purse for her car keys and headed toward the front door.

Within a few minutes, Dawn and Sarah had thanked the nurse, buckled Charity in her car seat, bade good-bye to Jeff, and turned onto the main thoroughfare toward Rocky Bluff. "Are you as hungry as I am?" Dawn asked her younger friend.

"With all the excitement about bringing little Charity home, I completely forgot about breakfast. I guess I am pretty hungry."

"There's a fast food drive-thru ahead. It won't be a gourmet meal, but it should hold us over until we get back to Rocky Bluff," Dawn replied as she slowed her car and turned it into the next drive.

❧

"Hey, Sarah, wait up," Ryder shouted as the political science class filed into the hallway and began to scatter in different directions.

Sarah turned at the sound of the familiar greeting as Ryder worked his way through the crowd of students. "You weren't in class yesterday and I was worried about Charity. How is she?"

"She appears fine. Her CAT scan didn't show any problems, and she didn't have any more symptoms of a seizure so we brought her home yesterday. I'm going to Little Lambs now, would you like to join me?"

"I'd love to," Ryder replied. "I've been so concerned about her that I even called Teresa Olson and asked her to start the church prayer chain."

Sarah smiled. "Their prayers must have been what did it, because in no time at all she was back to her same giggly self."

The harsh December wind whipped against their faces as

they stepped into the parking lot. They wrapped their scarves tightly around their necks and reached for their gloves in their pockets. "I'm parked at the far north end of the lot. Would you like to wait inside while I bring the car around?" Ryder suggested. "There's no need for both of us to freeze."

"Nah, I'm tough," Sarah laughed as they hurried across the parking lot together. The wind prevented conversation, but Sarah's mind continued to race. *Ryder's always thoughtful and concerned about others. The majority of the other guys in my classes seem self-absorbed and interested only in material possessions and recreation, but Ryder is different. He'll make a good physician's assistant and a good husband to some lucky woman.*

ᴥ

After the pair was settled in the warmth of Ryder's sports car and they had left the college parking lot, Sarah said, "What did you do in class yesterday? I hated to miss it. It was the first class I missed all semester, but I didn't have much of a choice. Some things just naturally take priority."

"Not much," Ryder replied as he smiled. He admired the vibrant glow in Sarah's cheeks caused by the biting cold. "We just reviewed for our test tomorrow."

"Oh, dear. I forgot all about it," Sarah gasped. "I really need to get a good grade on that test. Did you happen to take good notes?"

"You, worry?" Ryder teased. "Are you afraid you'll get an A minus instead of an A?" Noticing the panic in her eyes in the rearview mirror, he quickly changed his tone. "I took the best notes I could," he tried to assure her. "I didn't think I'd need them today so I left them home. After we leave Little Lambs, would you like to get a bite to eat at the Black Angus and then come to my house so we can study for the test together? That is. . .if my little brother will leave us alone.

He has a knack of turning up everyplace he's not welcome."

"I appreciate your offer. I dislike group projects intensely, but I seem to remember stuff so much better when I work with just one person and we can question each other back and forth without interruption," Sarah replied as her smile broadened. "I understand about little brothers. Only recently has Mark begun to show human characteristics."

That afternoon flew by as Sarah played with Charity, and Ryder played with several of the other children, helping them with their cognitive learning skills. Seeing Charity laughing and back to normal helped Sarah forget her dread of the upcoming test.

When it was the children's supper time, Sarah and Ryder hugged the children good-bye, retrieved their coats, and slipped into the dark, cold winter air. During the month of December in Montana, it was dark by 4:30 in the afternoon and city lights were ablaze when people got off work. The Christmas lights lit the city streets as they approached the Black Angus while Christmas carols echoed from the car radio. If it weren't for the nagging fear of the upcoming exam, Sarah would have claimed that the entire world was perfect.

For nearly an hour, the two students shared their mutual concerns about college and their future. Both were concerned that they would not get an A in all their classes. Ryder was extremely concerned about getting admitted to the University of Iowa and Sarah wanted to prove to herself that she could get good grades and become a role model for her daughter. As they cruised slowly down the street where Rebecca Hatfield lived, the surrounding houses were aglow with blinking lights while Rebecca's stood dark and sterile with only a single dim light and the reflection from the TV flickering through the window.

"It's kind of sad, isn't it?" Ryder noted. "The bleakness in her home seems to reflect the bleakness that is consuming her once vibrant life."

"I hope I'll be able to bring a little joy into her life when I move in," Sarah replied wistfully.

Glancing to his side, Ryder admired the attractive young woman beside him. He was inspired by the inner strength with which she faced the problems in her life and yet had the compassion and concern to reach out to the needs of others. "When do you plan to move in?"

"I'd like to move my stuff right after I finish my last test at the end of the term and then leave for Billings the same day," Sarah replied, "but I have a lot of details yet to work through."

"Do you have anyone to help you?"

"I've been so busy with Charity's problems that I haven't given it any consideration." A teasing twinkle entered Sarah's eyes. "Does that mean you're volunteering for the job?"

"You are extremely perceptive, Miss Brown," Ryder snickered back. "As soon as tests are over, your time is my time. In fact, if you need a ride to Billings, I'd be glad to give you a lift. I have an aunt living there whom I haven't seen in a couple of years. I'm sure I could spend the night with her before heading back."

"Yeh. . .sure," she readily agreed. "I never turn down help." Sarah was amazed at the kindness the people in Rocky Bluff had shown her since her daughter moved into Little Lambs Children's Center. Even before she enrolled in the community college, she had attended church every time she was in town and the congregation immediately embraced her with Christian love and understanding without judging her for her sinful past.

The remainder of the evening, the pair discussed the details of Sarah's move, from Ryder's borrowing a pickup, to where to obtain enough boxes to pack her personal items. After their plans were completed, Sarah finally said, "It's been a good evening, but I'm becoming extremely weary. Would you mind taking me home?"

"I'm sorry," Ryder replied as he glanced at his watch and pointed his car toward the campus. "I hadn't realized it was so late."

A relaxed peace settled upon them as he retraced his familiar path through the well-lit streets of Rocky Bluff. With Charity out of immediate danger, Sarah reminded herself of her ambivalent feelings toward developing a serious relationship with a man. Any man.

When the young couple arrived at the parking lot outside the women's dormitory, Ryder parked the car and escorted Sarah through the cold and blustery air. He wrapped his arm protectively around her and pulled her close to himself as she shuddered in the briskness of a December evening in Montana. When they reached the front door, Sarah looked up into his warm dark eyes to thank him for the delightful evening. As their eyes met, they locked. Slowly and silently, Ryder moved his lips toward hers, and instinctively Sarah pressed her lips against his.

After maintaining their embrace for several moments, Sarah pulled away. "Thank you for a lovely evening," she smiled. "I'll see you in class tomorrow."

"This evening was special for me. Would you mind if I join you tomorrow when you visit Charity?" Ryder asked.

"Please do," Sarah smiled as she disappeared behind the glass door of her dormitory.

When Sarah returned to her dorm room, she was anxious to obtain a few quiet moments to bask in the tenderness of the last few moments. However, her roommate, Vanessa, was eager to tell everyone about the date she just had with the quarterback of the football team.

"I had the greatest time tonight," Vanessa exclaimed. "Doug and I went to the Bobcat Grill for dinner and dancing. Several of his teammates showed up and asked me to dance as well. . . . I never had it so good. . .and to top it all off, I saw several of the cheerleaders there with nerdy guys. I'm sure they were green with jealousy."

"Sounds like fun," Sarah replied, trying to sound polite as her mind kept drifting back to the closeness she felt toward Ryder as compared with the stability and sense of history she shared with Jeff. Suddenly, the ringing of the telephone rudely interrupted their discussion.

"Hello," Sarah greeted as she brushed her long brown hair behind her ear.

"Hello. . . Is this Sarah?"

"Yes it is," she replied, trying to recognize the familiar voice.

"This is Beth Blair, Jeff's mother," a trembling voice replied. "I have some bad news for you."

Sarah's eyes widened. "What happened?"

"Jeff had an accident on his way back from Great Falls," the anxious mother explained, trying to maintain a calm exterior. "His car slid off the road when he hit a patch of ice coming down Rodger's Pass. I suppose it could have been a lot worse. Fortunately the car was stopped by a tree before he slid all the way to the bottom."

"Oh no," Sarah gasped. "Was he hurt?"

Beth explained the seriousness of Jeff's injuries. The young woman already had enough on her mind with her concern for little Charity and the intensity with which she took on her college studies. It was nearing final exam week and Sarah would need to focus all her attention on her finals and not Jeff's injuries.

"Jeff has four broken ribs, cracks to several disks in his back and bruises all over his body. He was fortunate that his neck was not broken. He'll be in the hospital for some time and then will require physical therapy for several more months after that."

ঝ

Sarah's mind raced as she imagined the father of her child lying in a hospital bed racked with pain. There had to be something she could do to help. "Beth, I want to come to Missoula to be with him," she exclaimed, "but I don't have the money and I have several tests and term papers due before the fourteenth."

"That's okay, dear," Beth tried to calm her. "Jeff will understand your concern, but truthfully, there's little you can do to help, except pray. He's in a lot of pain and needs to rest quietly to let his body heal itself. Some of the medicines he's taking make him sleep a lot, but I'll let him know of your concern when he wakes up."

"Beth, thank you for calling. If there's anything I can do, please let me know," Sarah took a deep breath and tried to sound brave, even though the lilt in her voice betrayed her weak confidence. "I'll notify the church prayer chain and ask them to pray for Jeff."

"I'll keep you updated on his progress," Beth promised. "Just leave Jeff in the hands of God and the doctors and focus on your schoolwork. You have a lot of things on your mind right now, and I don't want your grades to suffer."

"I'll do my best," Sarah assured her as she bade her farewell, hung up the telephone, and flopped across her bed.

Sarah lay quietly for several minutes with her face buried in her pillow. As if unable to withstand the silence, Vanessa sat on the corner of Sarah's bed and put her hand on Sarah's shoulder.

ಇಾ

Sarah was different from the other girls she knew. Sarah rarely talked about her past, but Vanessa gathered that she had been through much heartache that made her what she was today. Vanessa admired the inner strength and security of her roommate that seemed to come from her faith in Christ and the people in her church. She wanted to someday have the same peace that Sarah had, but right now, she was enjoying the fun she was having with her college friends. Vanessa did not want to take the time away from her friends to discover the source of Sarah's inner strength.

But now, when she needed a source of wisdom to comfort her roommate, Vanessa only felt an inner emptiness.

"I'm so sorry," Vanessa said, trying to comfort her roommate, but her voice trembled with lack of confidence. "There seems to be a lot of stuff swirling around in your head right now. Would you like to talk about it?"

"Maybe later," Sarah replied as she rolled over and forced a smile at her roommate. "Right now I just need a little time to pray and get my thoughts sorted out. Every time it looks like things are finally falling into place, something else happens."

Vanessa squeezed her roommate's hand. "I understand. I'll go down to the lounge to study for a while so you can be by yourself."

"Thanks," Sarah murmured as Vanessa slipped quietly out the door.

ಇಾ

The glow of the magical evening with Ryder faded into a faint memory. Sarah stared at the ceiling as she tried to remember each moment that she had had with Jeff. She remembered the reckless summer nearly four years ago when they had let down their guard and several weeks later when she discovered she was pregnant. She thought of the months he stood by her after she learned the baby would be born with birth defects. She admired his faithfulness of paying child support for the care of Charity at Little Lambs and the frequent visits he made to Rocky Bluff to visit her. She thought of the tenderness Jeff displayed when he held his daughter in his arms. She remembered the fun they had during the Thanksgiving Dinner at Little Lambs and the next day when they took their daughter to the mall to see the Christmas decorations. The thought of Jeff's strong, muscular body lying bruised and broken in a hospital bed in Missoula brought tears to her eyes. *I suppose his football days are over. If so, will he lose his football scholarship and have to drop out of college? Will he still be able to walk when he gets out of the hospital?*

Sarah tried praying, but she felt her prayers of desperation were not even reaching the ceiling of her dorm room. She tried reading comforting words from the Scripture, but her favorite passages did not contain their normal encouragement. She turned the radio on to a Christian music station, but the music could not cut through her pain. Feeling herself sinking deeper and deeper into despair, Sarah did what she often did when the pressures of life became overwhelming. She reached for the telephone and dialed Dawn Reynolds.

eight

Through a fog of pain, Jeff Blair stared at the ceiling tile in his hospital room. His neck brace felt like a vise, and his chest was encompassed in a modified body cast. He tried to remember the events of the last few hours, but drugs had dimmed his memory. "Jeff, how are you feeling?" a familiar voice queried.

The injured football player tried to turn his head to answer his mother, but the pain intensified. "Mom, I've never hurt this bad in my life. I can scarcely move. What happened?"

"Your car slid off Rodger's Pass and hit a tree," Beth replied as she brushed a lock of hair from his sweaty brow. "Even though you feel miserable right now, you're a mighty lucky man."

Jeff's weak voice became panicky. "Am I going to be all right?"

Beth took a deep breath as tears gathered in her eyes. "You have four broken ribs, cracks to several disks, and several torn ligaments," she explained. "You'll need to be in physical therapy for several months, but the doctors think there's a good chance you'll make a total recovery."

Jeff's already pale face whitened even more as he gulped. "You mean there's a chance I might not be able to walk again."

Beth patted his hand. "There are people all over the country praying for your complete recovery. We must trust that God will work a miracle on your behalf."

Jeff looked away and closed his eyes, trying not to let his

88

mother see the tears that threatened to spill. Jeff and his mother had always been close and he knew that she could sense his need for quiet, to let him work through his emotions. Jeff's first five years had been extremely difficult, and his mother had done everything she could to protect him from the harshness in life. Even after she had married Dan Blair, that same pattern persisted; but now there was nothing she could do but pray and encourage others to storm heaven with their prayers for Jeff.

❧

When Beth Slater was a teenager in Rocky Bluff, she had learned to depend on the Lord for both the minor and the most complicated issues of life. She had been a struggling single mother trying to care for her baby, Jeffey, when Dawn Reynolds's grandmother, Edith Harkness Dutton, took her under her wing. Edith not only provided motherly advice on how to care for a baby, but she also led Beth into an understanding and acceptance of the Christian faith. Edith had encouraged Beth to finish her high school education and become a financially self-supporting and capable, nurturing mother.

Edith had been Beth's stabilizing force during those traumatic days when little Jeffey's natural father had kidnapped him and taken him to Canada. Jeffey's return under the most difficult and unlikely circumstances had fully convinced her of the power of prayer. But now, as she sat vigil at her son's bedside, she again threw herself on the mercy of Christ for help.

❧

While his mother was struggling to maintain optimism and faith during a difficult situation, Jeff slowly slipped into periods of self-examination and questioning. *If I'm not able to play football, I'll lose my football scholarship and have to increase my hours at the Pizza Parlor. But then, if I can't stand*

for long periods at a time, I won't be able to make pizzas. . . .
If I started delivering pizzas I wouldn't be able to earn enough
to pay both tuition and child support.

Little Charity's innocent face flashed before him. Whatever the cost, he had to keep going, on her account. Her birth was totally unplanned and unintended. However, from the beginning it was obvious that God had a reason for her young life. Already, in the three short years of her life, she had been a witness of personal strength and determination.

During the first summer that he knew Sarah, he saw her only as a silly, shallow teenager. But through the years he had watched her change into a mature young woman striving hard to receive an education so that she could not only financially support her daughter, but also be able to care for the multitude of medical needs that Charity had.

The squeaking of the hospital door interrupted Jeff's moments of contemplation. "How are you doing?" a nurse inquired as she approached his bed.

Jeff tried to turn his head that was still constrained in a neck brace. He grimaced as pain engulfed his entire body. "I feel miserable," he moaned. "I hurt all over."

"This will help take the intensity of the pain away," the nurse replied as she held up a needle that appeared to be two feet long.

"At this point I'll accept about anything," Jeff retorted, trying to make a feeble attempt at humor to mask his pain and depression.

After the shot, Jeff was asleep within minutes and his mother slipped quietly from the hospital room. The hours at her son's bedside were taking a heavy toll on her body and every muscle seemed to cry out for sleep.

❧

For the next few hours, Jeff drifted in and out of consciousness.

Several times he was aware of his father's presence, but only mumbled a brief greeting before going back to sleep. He was never fully awake until the young assistant from the food service noisily set a tray on his table and loudly announced, "Good morning, Mr. Blair. Your breakfast is here."

Jeff opened his eyes and faked a weak smile. "Thank you," he murmured as he surveyed the tray of toast, cereal, fruit, and coffee. He ate slowly as his chest muscles seemed to shudder with each swallow. *At least there's less pain than yesterday, so I assume that's progress,* he told himself.

For the next two hours, Jeff's time was filled with doctor visits, nursing assistants taking care of his personal needs, and a mild workout with the physical therapist. When he was finally alone, he again drifted back into his state of self-absorption and reflection. *Will my injuries keep me from marrying?* He thought about his growing feelings toward Sarah. *What would it be like spending my entire lifetime with Sarah? If I would marry her, would it be because I truly love her or would it be because of my sense of duty for having fathered her child?*

The more Jeff's mind dwelled on Sarah's sweet smile and bubbly personality, the more he began to convince himself that he truly loved her. *If I would marry Sarah, would we have another disabled child?* he pondered. *It's generally thought that spina bifida is caused by the lack of folic acid in the mother's system during early pregnancy, but no one is one hundred percent sure of that fact. What if I am a carrier of a gene that causes birth defects? I don't know anything about my natural father's medical history. Maybe I shouldn't even think about marriage until I am certain it wouldn't happen again.*

Jeff stared at the ceiling without moving while he considered the complexity of his relationship with Sarah Brown.

He became more determined than ever that he had to find his natural father before he could consider a serious relationship with her or any other woman.

While Jeff was trapped in his intense soul-searching, his mother entered the room. "How are you doing today, dear?" Beth said as she leaned over and kissed her son on the forehead.

"I'm feeling a lot better today," he replied dryly. "However, I've been doing a lot of thinking." Jeff studied his mother's face, trying to figure out how to explain his dilemma without hurting the two people who had done so much for him. He took a deep breath, but even that slight motion caused pain.

"Mom," he began cautiously. "You know how much I love you and Dad. I wouldn't do anything in the world that would hurt you." Jeff hesitated, trying to search for the right words while Beth waited patiently. "I've been doing a lot of thinking about little Charity. She's such a precious child, but I'm concerned about what caused her neural tube deficiency. What if I'm carrying a defective gene that I could pass on to other children? I'm not sure that I should ever consider marriage if that is the case."

Beth took her son's hand and stroked his forehead. "Jeff, no one knows for sure what causes each individual birth defect. Right now it's more important that you concentrate on getting well. You can research the possible causes of spina bifida when you get out of the hospital."

"Mother, you don't understand," he persisted. "I need to know my natural father's medical history before I even consider any kind of relationship with a woman. I don't want to be accused of leading a girl on and then dropping her just when it appears that we might become serious. Sarah doesn't deserve any more pain in her life."

"In this case, I don't agree with you," Beth replied kindly. "If a young woman truly loves a person, she'll accept him, regardless of what his medical history may be. . . . However, I understand why you feel the way you do. . . . Is there anything I can do to help?"

Jeff squeezed his mother's hand. She had stood by him every moment in his life and now she was again willing to uphold him. "Mom, what do you know about my natural father? Do you know where I might locate him?"

Beth gulped and her face blanched. "Truthfully, I know very little about him and haven't heard anything about him since he went to jail in Canada after he kidnapped you when you were four years old. His name is Mickey Kilmer. He grew up in Elders Point, Montana. After he learned I was pregnant with his child, he joined the Marines. However, his military career didn't last long and he received a bad conduct discharge for wrongful use and possession of a controlled substance."

"Do you know what happened to him after he left the Marines?" Jeff queried.

Beth shook her head. "I completely lost track of Mickey until he turned up in Rocky Bluff in a black Porsche and took you from the day care."

"I faintly remember that," Jeff replied. "I was really impressed with his fancy car, but I couldn't understand why he didn't take me back to you when I started crying. I think I cried nonstop for three days."

"There was a massive search for you and your picture as a missing child even ended up on milk cartons in all the states of the Northwest and in Canada. Several weeks later, the Royal Canadian Mounted Police arrested Mickey for possession of two kilos of cocaine and an illegal handgun and who knows what else. I think he was sentenced to ten years in prison, but he could have gotten out in four to five for good behavior. I'm not sure."

Jeff shook his head with disgust. "He must have been some wild dude."

The furrows on Beth's forehead deepened as she tried to remain calm. "Knowing that your natural father was in jail for drugs, are you certain you want to locate him? You may not like what you find."

"Because of his more antisocial behavior it makes it even more imperative that I find him," Jeff stated firmly. "That means it's even more likely that I might have a genetic defect in my background. Maybe he has a serious mental illness or something. I could be a genetic time bomb waiting to explode."

"Jeff, I think you're having too much time on your hands to think," Beth scolded good-naturedly. "You're letting your imagination get the better of you."

Jeff remained silent for a few minutes, frustrated at his mother's response. "Mother, I don't think you understand how important this is to me," he said quietly. "If I'm ever to marry, I have to know my medical background."

Beth shook her head. "Like I said before, I'll do whatever I can to help you find your natural father," she repeated. "However, there's not much more I can tell you. . . . When Dan and I were married, an attorney in Rocky Bluff named Stuart Leonard made arrangements through a Canadian attorney to have your natural father sign papers surrendering all custody rights to you. As soon as the paperwork was completed, Dan was able to legally adopt you and he raised you as if you were his natural-born son."

Jeff's eyes filled with tears. "It's hard to imagine what my life would have been like if Dan Blair hadn't adopted me. He's been the best father imaginable."

"I have to admit, my entire life changed when Dan Blair entered my life," Beth replied. "Edith Harkness Dutton helped me get my life together and then Dan accepted my with all me warts and blemishes and he readily accepted you as if you were his own son."

"He made me feel so special at your wedding, the way he included me," Jeff replied with his customary twinkle reappearing in his eyes. "It took me a long time to figure out that not all kids got to be a part of their parents' wedding."

Jeff and his mother continued discussing their early years alone together for another hour. With each passing sentence, Jeff became more and more determined to find Mickey Kilmer. Their conversation ended when the cafeteria assistant delivered the noon meal, and Beth excused herself to have lunch in the hospital cafeteria.

As Jeff ate his meatloaf and vegetables, his mind drifted back to his daughter, Charity, and her mother. How he wanted to pursue a mature romance with Sarah Brown, but until he knew the truth of his background, he was afraid to do so. Ironically, just as he was thinking about her, the phone beside his bed rang. Painfully, he reached to answer it.

"Hello."

"Hello. . .is that you, Jeff?"

The pain of stretching his sore muscles faded as he recognized the voice of the very person he was thinking about. "Yes. Is this Sarah?"

"Yes it is," she replied cautiously. "I wanted to check on how you were doing, so I called your house to talk with your mother, but no one answered. I thought she would probably be at the hospital with you and would answer the phone. This is a thrill to actually hear your voice."

"Mom's down in the cafeteria, eating right now, and I'm just lying here indulging in this fantastic hospital food," Jeff chuckled weakly.

"So how are you doing? I was stunned to learn of your accident."

"I'm feeling a lot better than I did a couple of days ago," Jeff admitted, "but I still have a long way to go. I'll have to have physical therapy for several months and right now I don't know if I'll ever be able to walk normally again."

"What. . .what. . .will you do if you can't walk? Will you still be able to go to school? What will happen to your football scholarship?" Sarah stammered.

Jeff wanted to share his inner fears and frustrations, but he didn't want to let her know how much she meant to him. That was. . .not until he knew the truth about his background, and then he would be able to bare his soul to her. "The buildings are all handicapped accessible, but financing my education could become a real challenge," he replied with fake confidence. "I'm sure something will work out. Mom says a lot of people are praying for me."

The two talked for several minutes, but Jeff's responses became shorter and more abrupt as he struggled between wanting to share openly with Sarah and being afraid he would lose his determination to find his father's medical records.

Sarah detected a distance and coolness in his voice that she had never heard before. Her first instinct was to feel hurt, but then she tried to rationalize, *I've never heard him sound so aloof and disinterested before, even when we talked about Charity. He must be in a lot of pain.*

"Are you getting too tired to talk?" Sarah queried.

"Not especially."

"Oh," Sarah responded weakly. "Your voice was becoming weak."

Jeff hesitated. "I was just looking at my lunch and thinking how cold it was becoming."

Sarah's voice cracked. "I'd better let you get back to your lunch. I'll keep you in my prayers."

"Thanks," he murmured as he hung up the phone.

Tears welled up in Jeff's eyes. It had been so difficult not to tell Sarah how frightened he was of the future and the fear that engulfed him that he might not be able to keep up his child support payments. If only he knew that he could not pass any birth defects or serious illnesses on to his future children, he would let Sarah know how much he loved her.

❧

Sarah and Ryder had just finished their last test of the semester and hurried across campus to the women's dormitory. The halls were a flurry of students, their parents and boyfriends carrying boxes from each of the rooms. Sarah pushed her key into the keyhole. Her roommate's possessions were stacked on one side of the room and hers on the other.

"With this mess, I don't even know where to begin," Sarah sighed.

"One box at a time," Ryder chuckled. "Just make sure you keep the suitcases you're going to take with you to Billings separate. That would cause all kinds of frustrations going through Christmas break without the things you need."

For the next half hour, Sarah and Ryder carried all Sarah's earthly belongings to Ryder's borrowed pickup truck. When Sarah's half of the room was empty, they each picked up the suitcases that she was planning to take home with her, locked the door, and left the key at the front desk.

"We'll have to hurry and unload," Ryder exclaimed as he slid behind the wheel of the truck. "I told my friend I'd be done by two o'clock so he could move his girlfriend's stuff."

"It shouldn't take us too long," Sarah replied. "Teresa Olson said she would be waiting for us at Rebecca Hatfield's. She offered to help us unload so we can leave for Billings as soon as possible."

Ryder turned the borrowed truck out of the college parking

lot and onto a main street as Sarah took one long look at the dormitory. Even though she would be attending classes for one more semester, she would no longer be living on campus. Her life seemed to be always in a state of change.

"How has Rebecca been doing lately?" Ryder queried, unable to imagine what it would be like living with and caring for someone with Alzheimer's.

"Teresa said she has her good days and her bad days, but that the bad days are becoming more and more frequent. I just hope I'm up to the challenge."

"I'm sure you will be," Ryder assured her. "You seem to have a real knack for taking care of the sick and disabled. Sometimes I wonder why you don't train for a medical career instead of computers."

Sarah thought a moment. "I've seriously considered it," she replied. "However, I get too emotionally involved with those I try to help. I don't think I'd be able to maintain the professional distance necessary to make objective decisions for patients."

nine

Jeff Blair rose from the wheelchair, took his walker, and stepped into the cold December air. After more than three weeks of lying in a hospital bed and going through hours of grueling physical therapy, he was now ready to go home. For days, his family had hoped and prayed that Jeff would be able to be home for Christmas; and now their prayers were finally answered when the doctor signed his release form on the twenty-fourth of December. In spite of the hours the family had spent at the hospital sitting by Jeff's bedside, they had found time to put up the Christmas decorations, and gifts were piled high beneath the tree. An aura of praise, anticipation, and thanksgiving filled the house.

Jeff finally had accepted the fact that with intense physical therapy, he would probably be able to walk again on his own, but would never have the agility that he once had. However, now he was so excited to be going home that he did not consider his long-range plans. His father helped him into the backseat of the car, and then folded his walker, and placed it in the trunk. Jeff's little sister, Edith, greeted him excitedly while their mother smiled proudly at her offspring from the front seat.

As soon as Jeff arrived home, instead of going directly to the refrigerator, which was his custom, he went to the computer in the office. "Gee, it's good to see you again," he chuckled as he patted the monitor.

"You're just as weird as you ever were," Edith teased as she followed her brother into the office, as if not wanting to admit how excited she was to have her older brother home again.

"Pardon me, little Sis," Jeff said as he sat down and booted up the computer, "but I have some serious research to do."

"What kind of research is it?" Edith persisted. "You haven't started back to school yet and your teachers have all given you an extension on your course work. Usually your research consists of the contents of the refrigerator."

"I just want to use the people finder on the Internet. Now, why don't you go play. . .and on your way you might bring me back a can of pop."

"You haven't changed a bit," the thirteen-year-old retorted lightly as she left the room, ignoring his request for a soft drink.

As soon as his sister was gone, Jeff located a people finder on the Internet and typed in Mickey Kilmer. Much to his surprise, three different addresses appeared on the screen—one in Albany, Georgia, one in Portland, Maine, and one in Spokane, Washington. He copied the three addresses onto his hard drive and then printed them out. Two of the addresses provided E-mail addresses.

Jeff then wrote the same message to the Mickey Kilmer in Georgia and the one in Maine.

Dear Mickey:

I am trying to locate the Mickey Kilmer who was born in Elders Point, Montana, approximately forty years ago. Could you be that person?

Jeff Blair
Missoula, Montana

The entire process took Jeff a little over fifteen minutes. After shutting down the computer, Jeff took his walker and inched his way toward the kitchen. He was thankful to be home and as independent as he was, but extremely frustrated that he could not move faster.

Beth Blair was standing in front of the open refrigerator when Jeff entered. "You have that 'I need a can of pop' look on your face," she chuckled as she reached into the refrigerator.

"Thanks, Mom," Jeff replied as he took a chair at the kitchen table. "You always could read my mind."

"That comes with being a mother," she laughed as she gave him a quick hug. "Since it's your first night home, I'll give you a choice for what we'll have. But if I know you, you'll probably select spaghetti."

Jeff's eyes sparkled as he responded to his mother's squeeze. "That's exactly right," he agreed and then his expression became serious. "Who did you say was the attorney who handled my adoption?"

"Stuart Leonard," Beth replied, unable to hide her puzzlement. "He should be getting close to retirement age by now. I don't know if he's still in Rocky Bluff or not."

Jeff took a sip of his soft drink and then set the can on the table beside him. "I think I'll call Dawn Reynolds and see if she knows anything about him. Besides, I want to check to see how Charity is doing. I haven't heard anything for a couple of weeks." Jeff took a worn slip of paper from his wallet and reached for the cordless phone on the wall beside him.

In a few moments, the director of Little Lambs Children's Center was answering the phone with a cheery "Merry Christmas."

"Hello, Dawn, this is Jeff Blair," the young man greeted. "I just wanted to call and wish you a Merry Christmas and to see how Charity is doing. Has she had any more seizures?"

"Charity is doing remarkably well," Dawn assured him. "And there have not been any more seizures. I hope the one she had last Thanksgiving was an isolated event. The only bad thing is that since Sarah has gone home to Billings a few days ago, she seems so sad. Every so often she'll say, 'When's Mommy coming? When's Mommy coming?' "

"I wish I were there to hold her," Jeff sighed, "but I'm glad she's doing better and that Sarah has a chance to go back to Billings. She's been working much too hard—she needed a vacation." Every time he heard Sarah's name, a corner of his soul seemed to jump for joy.

"How are you doing?" Dawn queried. "I know it's been a long haul for you."

Jeff took a deep breath. He had a reputation of always being jovial and on top of the world, able to mask his inner fears and doubts. However, after three weeks of intense self-examination he was no longer able to live behind his superficial mask. "They finally let me out of the hospital this afternoon," Jeff explained, "but I'm not getting around too well. I'm afraid I'm going to be in physical therapy for a long while and I don't have any assurances that I'll ever be able to run again."

"I'm sorry to hear that," Dawn replied in a tone expressing her deep compassion for another's suffering. "I'll be remembering you in my prayers," she assured him. "If there's anything else I can do for you, please feel free to ask."

Jeff hesitated. "Well. . .er. . .there is one thing."

"What's that?" Dawn queried.

"Do you know if there is still an attorney in town by the name of Stuart Leonard?"

"Yes, I see him at church quite often," Dawn replied. "He's semi-retired now and I think he only takes social security cases. Why do you ask?"

"Mother says that he was the one who handled my adoption and was able to get my natural father to give up all parental rights so Dan could adopt me. I want to find my natural father so that I can learn more about my medical background."

Dawn hesitated. "Jeff, are you afraid there might be genetic complications that were aggravated by your injury?"

"Oh no, it has nothing to do with my own health," he replied hastily. "I just want to make sure that I'm not carrying any gene that would lead to serious birth defects or mental illness. How do I know that Charity's spina bifida wasn't caused by a gene I was carrying?"

"Jeff, no one knows the exact cause of spina bifida, so right now all we can do is accept the fact it happened and help Charity live life to its fullest potential," Dawn insisted.

"But what if I'm carrying a bad gene? I shouldn't have any more children," Jeff persisted. "In fact, I really shouldn't even consider marriage. And if I can't consider marriage, I shouldn't show much interest in girls because they might mistake my kindness for something more serious, and then they will only be hurt."

Jeff's words tumbled out one on top of another while Dawn listened patiently. "Is there one girl in particular that you're afraid of hurting?"

Sarah's intense hazel eyes and innocent face flashed before him. He had already caused her enough pain in her life, he could not think of causing any more. "Dawn, to be honest with you, I'm beginning to see Sarah in a totally different light. She's no longer that silly teenager working in a pizza parlor in Billings, but she is one of the most intelligent, compassionate women I've ever met. I don't want to even consider a serious relationship with her until I know for sure that I'm not carrying a bad gene."

Dawn hesitated, as she again searched for the right words of comfort. "Jeff, no child enters this world without God's planning. As sad as it is to see little Charity's deformities, you have already seen all the joy she has brought to so many people's lives. You cannot live a life of fear and deny yourself love because of what might, or might not, happen. Life can't exist on 'what-ifs,' but on faith and trust in God."

Jeff paused. He knew Dawn was right; he was letting his fear get the better of him. However, before he could respond, Dawn continued, "Jeff, whenever I'm feeling discouraged I always go back to the Bible in Proverbs 3:5–6. 'Trust in the Lord with all thine heart; and lean not unto thine own understanding. In all thy ways acknowledge him, and he shall direct thy paths.' "

"Dawn, to tell you the truth, I have done a lot of soul-searching while I was lying in the hospital. Things that used to seem so important, no longer seem important at all and the things I've always taken for granted are now extremely precious to me. I've always loved my family, but now I realize how lacking my love toward them has been," Jeff confessed.

Dawn's thoughts turned back to the time she struggled through her own period of soul-searching. She remembered her early years of college when she became more interested in partying and having a good time than she was in studying. Her social drinking had led to problem drinking, then to marijuana use, and finally to experimentation with cocaine. After being arrested at a party, along with several of her college friends, Dawn had spent several weeks in the Rimrock Rehabilitation Center in Billings. During that period she too did a lot of soul-searching and then returned to a right relationship with her family and, most importantly, with her God.

"Jeff, I've been through many struggles similar to what you are going through," Dawn reminded him. "If there's ever anything I can do or if you just need someone to listen, remember that I'm always available. If necessary, call me collect, even if it's in the middle of the night."

Dawn seemed to be the first person that understood the inner struggles he was going through. To him, everyone else listened politely, but their eyes betrayed their lack of understanding. Jeff relaxed as he continued to confide in her. "There is one thing that would help me," he said meekly. "After Christmas would you try to contact Stuart Leonard and ask him if he would be able to contact the Canadian officials and help me locate Mickey Kilmer? Also, would you ask him what his fee would be? I hope I can afford him. Now that I can't stand for long periods of time, I'm going to have to give up my current part-time job and find another."

"I'll be happy to try to contact Stuart," Dawn replied, "but I may have to wait until after the first of the year. A lot of the professionals in town are taking extended vacations over the holidays."

Finally finding someone who he thought understood his plight, Jeff's spirits began to lift. He did not want to have to break off his friendship with Sarah, at least not until he knew the truth of his background. However, relieved that Dawn was going to help with his search, Jeff gained the confidence to call Sarah in Billings to reassure her of their friendship and wish her a Merry Christmas.

***

Three o'clock January 2, Doris Brown stopped their family car in front of Rebecca Hatfield's home. "This is it," she said as tears began to build in her eyes. "We had a great vacation together and it's hard to say good-bye, but you have to get on with your life."

Sarah leaned over and hugged her mother. "Thanks for everything you've done for me. I just hope I can live up to everyone's expectations. I've never been around anyone with Alzheimer's before."

"I'm certain you'll do just fine," her mother assured her.

"Just make sure you get enough rest and eat properly. You'll need all the strength you can get."

Sarah gave her mother another hurried hug as she smiled at her familiar admonition to be sure and take care of herself. Sarah then got out of the car, took her suitcases from the trunk, took a deep breath, and walked up the front sidewalk. Although Teresa Olson had given her a front door key to Rebecca's home, Sarah felt it wiser not to startle Rebecca by using it and rang the doorbell instead.

A short matronly woman whom Sarah did not know opened the door. "Hello," she greeted, "may I help you?"

Sarah gulped. Whoever this person was she didn't know anything about her coming. "Hello," she responded. "I'm Sarah Brown. I'm going to be living with Rebecca for the next few months."

"I'm sorry. I should have recognized you," the woman replied kindly. "Do come in. They told me you were coming late this afternoon, but I wasn't expecting you so soon. My name is Ellen Booth, and I'm only here on weekends."

Ellen helped Sarah carry her suitcases to her bedroom. "Rebecca's been sleeping for over an hour, so I'm expecting her to wake up any time. She's been having a few more problems lately and the doctor has changed her medication."

"What's been wrong?" Sarah asked as she laid her suitcase on the bed and then followed the home health care worker back to the living room. "Is there anything different I should do for her than what I was told before Christmas?"

Ellen took a seat on the sofa and motioned Sarah to join her. "The only thing I can suggest is to be prepared for more of the unexpected. Her moods seem to be vacillating a lot more from happy and complacent to angry and cantankerous. She does not adapt well to anything out of the routine." Ellen gave a dry smile. "For example, never sit in her recliner. It takes her several hours to calm down from even the simplest disruption in the routine."

"Does she remember that I'm going to be staying here?" Sarah queried.

"I've told her several times today that you'd be coming, but I'm not sure she fully understands. I'll stay a little later than normal so she gets used to your presence," Ellen promised. "Teresa Olson said she'd be here in the morning before you have to go to class so Rebecca won't have to be by herself."

"A dietician plans her meals, allowing for certain flexibility. She stops by each week to check on the grocery needs and does the shopping," Ellen explained. "Those records are kept on the inside cupboard door over the dishwasher. An emergency call list is posted beside the telephone."

"Every possible need seems to be mapped out with extreme detail and forethought," Sarah noted, trying not to sound overwhelmed by her new job.

"Rebecca has contributed a lot to this community," Ellen replied, "and this is the least the people of Rocky Bluff could do to show their appreciation. In a lot of communities, she would have been in a nursing home six months ago. Rebecca is terrified to go to a nursing home, so everyone is doing their best to keep her home as long as possible."

"How much longer do they think she'll be able to stay in her own home?" Sarah asked.

Ellen shook her head sadly. "I personally think that if she can make it until June, we'll be extremely fortunate."

Suddenly, they heard shuffling in the hallway. "Rebecca," Ellen called out. "We're in the kitchen. Would you like to come and join us?"

The older woman entered the kitchen and took the nearest chair at the table. A pillow crease still left an indention on her wrinkled cheek. "Who are you?" she asked sharply as she noticed Sarah standing over the sink.

"I'm Sarah Brown," she began softly as she smiled and extended her hand. "I'm a student at the community college. I'm going to be staying with you for a few months and helping with some of your chores."

Rebecca took the young girl's hand and smiled. "I like having company, especially at night. Do you like to cook spaghetti? That's my favorite food."

"That's a coincidence," Sarah replied as she took the chair beside Rebecca. "That's my favorite food as well."

"What other foods do you like?" Sarah asked, trying to make small talk with her.

"Spaghetti is the only food I like," Rebecca replied dryly.

"You must eat other foods besides spaghetti," Sarah responded, unsure how to handle her first unclear conversation with Rebecca.

"People try to make me eat other stuff, but I won't do it regardless of what they say. You won't try to make me eat weird stuff, will you?"

Realizing that the first few hours they were together would be critical to their relationship, Sarah tried to think of something they could do together without being confrontational. Remembering one of the details that Ellen had just told her, Sarah said, "I understand that you like to put together jigsaw puzzles. Would you like me to set up the card table so we can work on one together?"

Rebecca's eyes brightened. "I'd love to. I'll show you where the card table is and I'll get my favorite puzzle. It has a really pretty mountain scene on it."

Ellen finished cleaning the kitchen and stayed in the background while Sarah began building a relationship with Rebecca. She made a light supper of grilled cheese sandwiches and soup.

When Rebecca looked at her plate she said, "Where's my spaghetti? I won't eat anything but spaghetti."

Sarah took a deep breath. "Let's close our eyes and pretend the toast is one large piece of spaghetti and the cheese is the sauce."

"That's silly," Rebecca retorted.

"Try it and see if they don't taste the same," Sarah replied as she closed her eyes and took a bite of her toast.

Much to Sarah's surprise, Rebecca copied her actions and then said. "You're right. It does taste like spaghetti."

From that point on, Rebecca ate her meal without complaint, while Sarah and Ellen exchanged knowing glances.

After the three women had eaten and the kitchen was tidied, Ellen turned to Sarah. "It looks like you have a handle on everything now, so I think I'll take this time to slip out. If you have any questions, just call me. My number is over the telephone."

Sarah stood to walk her to the door while Rebecca followed slowly behind them. "Good-bye, Ellen," Rebecca said. "Thanks for coming. I think I'll ask Sarah to spend the night with me to keep me company."

Ellen and Sarah exchanged knowing looks and smiled. "You're on your own now," Ellen said. "I'm sure you'll do a good job."

"Thanks," Sarah replied. "Just be sure and keep us in your prayers."

ten

Jeff Blair slid out from behind the wheel of his newly purchased, ten-year-old Ford and leaned against the car as he opened the back door. He removed his walker and breathed a sigh of relief to be able to bear his weight with his arms. He had just completed his first week back in class after his accident, and was beginning to understand the reason for the federal law requiring all buildings to be handicapped accessible.

Jeff hurried inside his home and went immediately to the office. He had so much schoolwork he needed to do. The mental struggle of starting a new semester while he was finishing projects and exams from the last semester was extremely challenging, but he was determined to make it. He had just become comfortable behind the computer when the phone rang.

"Hello."

"Hello. Is this Jeff?"

"Yes, it is."

"Hi, Jeff, this is Dawn Reynolds," the director of Little Lambs Children's Center replied. "Neither Sarah nor I had heard from you since before Christmas and we were wondering how you were doing."

"Physically I'm doing better, but I still need the walker for anything more than four steps," he replied, "but mentally I'm bushed. There's so much work to get done and so little time to do it in. I just hope I get all my course work made up before my extension runs out. I don't want to have to repeat any classes." The tone in Jeff's voice left no doubt as to the academic stress he was under.

"I wanted to bring you up-to-date on Charity's progress," Dawn continued. "She had one mild seizure earlier this week, but, after it was over, she was able to sleep it off and had no signs of side effects or physical damage."

Jeff's chin dropped as his forehead wrinkled. "Since she had a second one, will she have to go on seizure medication?" he asked, wishing he could be more involved in the day-to-day care of his child.

"Not at this time," Dawn replied. "Outside of those two bad episodes, Charity is doing remarkably well. We have a little computer at the center where the children can play storybooks on CD-ROM and they can interact with the story using the mouse. She just loves it and has trouble sharing it with the others."

Jeff smiled at the thought of his daughter's using a computer, and he remembered how at Thanksgiving time Charity would let go of the musical keyboard scarcely long enough for the clerk to scan the price. "Like I've said before," he laughed, "we have a budding genius on our hands."

"No doubt in my mind." Dawn laughed and then lowered her voice. "I do have some bad news for you," she began. "Stuart Leonard is going to be away in Arizona until the first of April, so I won't be able to see if he can trace Mickey Kilmer. I know how much finding him means to you, but it looks like we're dead-ended for a few months."

Jeff's eyes lowered as his mind wandered. "I still have a couple more things I could do," he finally murmured. "According to the people finder on the Internet there is a Mickey Kilmer living in Spokane, but it only gives a post office box for an address. I called directory assistance for a telephone number and was told that his number was unpublished. My next step would be to go to Spokane and try to find him, but

I won't be able to do that until I'm a little more steady on my twos."

Fortunately, Jeff couldn't see Dawn shaking her head on the other end of the telephone line. "That might be like finding a needle in a haystack. Spokane is a pretty large city for that," she reminded him. "What is your other option?"

"I could make a trip to Elders Point and ask around town and see if any of his family or old friends have heard from him recently," Jeff replied. "The problem with that action is that, even though it's still in Montana, Elders Point is nearly six hundred miles away. I won't be able to go there until summer vacation."

"It looks like either way, it will be awhile before you'll have an answer to your search." Dawn scolded teasingly as she continued, "I hope you're not intentionally going to withdraw from the female species until you find your natural father."

Jeff laughed, trying to mask his frustrations. "Nothing like that. Believe it or not, I've actually been too busy for any kind of social life. How has Sarah been doing lately?"

For a few moments, Dawn was lost for words. She would like to see the pair eventually marry and provide a stable home for their daughter, but a marriage to the wrong person, or when either one was not ready, would be totally devastating. "Taking care of someone with Alzheimer's has been extremely challenging for her, but she's doing an excellent job. Why don't you call her direct?" Then she gave him Sarah's number.

Jeff hurriedly scribbled the number on a piece of scrap paper lying on the desk. He continued his conversation with Dawn for a few more minutes then bade her good-bye and hung up the phone. *Maybe I should give Sarah a call. I really do miss her and it will probably be a long while before I know my full medical background,* he tried to justify to himself.

Surely, a simple phone call couldn't be construed as leading her on. Before I give her a call I'd better get me a can of pop from the refrigerator; it could be a long conversation.

Jeff took a chair at the kitchen table where he opened his soft drink. Just as he took his first sip, his mother burst through the front door with more exuberance than he had seen in her in a long time. "Jeff, I have some great news," she exclaimed as she threw her coat over a kitchen chair and took the seat next to him. "I talked to your physical therapist today and there is a new treatment that might help your injuries. They're not equipped to do it in Missoula yet, but they already have the equipment and training in a hospital in Spokane. She said she could arrange for you to go there within a month, but you'd have to stay there for over a week. If this treatment helps you, then they would have an even stronger argument to help convince the hospital board to purchase it for this hospital. I promised her that I'd talk with you this evening."

"Of course. . .I'll try anything," Jeff replied cheerfully. "However, I won't be able to go until after I've finished my work from last semester. I should be done in another week."

"Why don't you call her and set up a time?" Beth suggested.

Jeff reached for the kitchen phone and dialed the hospital number. After being switched between three different stations in the hospital, he finally was connected to the physical therapy department. The receptionist promptly informed him that the therapist was with a patient, but she would take his name and number and get back to him as soon as she was free. Jeff hung up the phone dejectedly. That meant he had to keep the telephone line open for the therapist's call and would not be able to call Sarah.

&

"Wait up, Sarah," Ryder Long shouted as he sprinted across

campus to catch up with her. "I haven't had a chance to talk with you since you came back from Christmas break."

"Sorry about that," Sarah replied. "I've been super busy keeping up with my class work, taking care of little Charity, and now Rebecca. I didn't realize taking care of someone with Alzheimer's would be so tasking."

"Do you have some time to tell me about it?" Ryder queried as he studied the dark circles under her eyes. "I'd love to buy you a soft drink or cup of coffee in the Commons."

The thought of having a few minutes to relax with a friend was extremely inviting. She was beginning to discover that in the midst of her caregiving to others, she was neglecting to care for her own emotional needs. "Sure, I'd love to," she replied. "I have another hour before I catch the shuttle downtown to see Charity."

The two hurried to the Commons in the next building to get out of the biting wind. Ryder purchased two soft drinks, and the pair found a booth in the far back corner.

Ryder studied Sarah's drawn face. "Is something bothering you? You haven't been the same for several days."

Tears welled up in her eyes. "It's like walking on eggshells when I'm with Rebecca Hatfield," Sarah confessed. "Everything that happens is my fault."

Ryder reached across the table and patted her on the hand. "I know it must be difficult."

"Just last night Rebecca couldn't find her slippers and she was certain that I had stolen them," Sarah explained as she wiped a tear from her eye. "I found them an hour later under her bed, but by that time she'd forgotten all about her outrage or even her desire for her slippers."

"It must be extremely hard to be wrongly accused of something and not be able to explain reality so that she can understand it," Ryder said, as he searched for words of comfort. "It must be kind of like when Jesus was falsely accused of all kinds of things, but He said nothing."

Sarah's eyes brightened. "I never thought of it in that manner. . .but what I feel is only like a grain of sand compared to what Christ must have felt."

"I certainly understand why you feel like you're walking on eggshells," Ryder said, trying to reaffirm his understanding of her internal conflict.

Sarah took a deep breath. "When something happens one time, it brings her great pleasure, and the next time she becomes angry with me and everything around her," she sighed. "I never know how she's going to react. One minute she's smiling and happy and the next she's shouting and extremely cantankerous. It takes a lot of patience not to react and take her criticism personally. Sometimes I question my own wisdom in how I handle certain situations."

"I'm certain you're doing an excellent job," Ryder tried to assure her. "I'm sure one of the hardest parts of the job is not having the confirmation and assurance from anyone that you have done the right thing."

Sarah's eyes became misty again. "You said exactly what I've been feeling, except I've been unable to put my feelings into words. I appreciate your listening to my frustrations. I don't seem to have time to talk with anyone lately."

Ryder reached over and took the young woman's hand. "With the heavy burden you are carrying, you need someone objective to confide in on a regular basis. How about meeting here at the same time every day after class and just unloading on me for a few minutes? It would probably do you a world of good."

Sarah smiled. "I usually have a half hour between my last class and when I catch the shuttle. It would be nice having someone my own age to talk with for a while. I'm either listening to lectures, talking kid talk with Charity, or trying to keep Rebecca connected with the day-to-day world the rest of the time."

As the days passed, Sarah found herself more and more looking forward to the short meetings with Ryder. Those few minutes together helped her gain a different perspective on the complexities of her life. But a faint gnawing seemed to be always with her as well. *I'm beginning to miss Jeff's sense of humor.*

❧

Knowing there was a chance for a different type of therapy, one that might possibly improve his condition, Jeff increased his hours of study even more. As soon as he completed all his work from the previous semester, he would be able to go to Spokane for a few days for treatment. Perhaps while he was there he might find some leads as to the Mickey Kilmer who lived in that city.

The day before Jeff's therapy was to begin, Dan Blair drove his son to the Spokane Medical Center. During the two-and-a-half-hour drive between Missoula and Spokane, Jeff and Dan had the most intense father-son talk they had ever had.

"I hope you're not offended by my trying to find my biological father," Jeff began, after they had left the outskirts of the city.

"Of course not," Dan replied as he glanced at his handsome son beside him. "It's very natural for a child to know as much about his past as possible. Finding your biological father will never erase the years of enjoyment we have had together."

A smile spread across Jeff's face. "Thanks, Dad," he replied. "You'll never know how much I've grown to love and respect you."

"The feeling is totally mutual," Dan replied. "In some ways, I kind of feel sorry for Mickey Kilmer. He could have had those parenting joys himself, but he chose to walk away from one of the greatest experiences of life—that of being a father."

After sharing several special father-son memories, the pair fell into a relaxed silence. Jeff tried to think of ways he might be able to locate Mickey Kilmer. *If he owned property, would I be able to find information at the county courthouse? Would I be able to get his address from a car registration? Would I be able to get an address from a credit report?* The more Jeff tried to think of ways to locate Mickey, the more concerned he became that some of his ideas were in violation of a person's right to privacy and he might never find his natural father.

Dan and Jeff checked into the motel across the street from the hospital and then went to dinner in a nearby restaurant. As soon as Jeff completed his series of therapy sessions, Dan planned to return to Spokane and drive Jeff home. Dan wished he could stay with his son longer, but the winter months were his busiest season at the Missoula Crisis Center, and he felt he had no other option.

By the second day of his therapy, Jeff was becoming extremely discouraged. His muscles did not seem to do what was expected of them, and some of the movements were extremely painful. Just when he was beginning to question the wisdom of taking time from his college studies, a voice echoed over the speaker system, "Paging Mickey Kilmer. . . Would Mickey Kilmer please report to the conference room?"

Jeff turned to his therapist. "Janet, does a Mickey Kilmer work for this hospital?"

"I think he's one of the maintenance men," the therapist replied, "do you know him?"

Jeff nodded as his mind began to race. "I'm not sure. I've

been trying to locate a Mickey Kilmer who used to live in Montana, but it could just be a coincidence. I found two others over the Internet, but neither one was the one I was trying to find. Is there some way I could meet this Mickey?"

Janet thought a moment and then went to her desk and dialed a number. "Hello, Adam. This is Janet up in Physical Therapy. I have a patient here who would like to meet Mickey Kilmer. Do you think you could arrange it?"

"I don't see a problem with that," the head of maintenance replied. "Mickey gets off work at three o'clock and has to stop here to check out. I'll ask him to wait until your patient gets here."

"Thanks. I appreciate your help," Janet replied, hung up the phone, and relayed the message to Jeff.

With the hope of finally meeting the Mickey Kilmer of Spokane, Jeff was able to ignore his pain while his muscles became energized. *Will this be the end of my search, or will I be disappointed once again?* he wondered. My biological father working in this hospital is just too much of a coincidence.

Ten minutes before three o'clock, Jeff entered the maintenance area of the hospital. He spoke to the head of the department, who pointed him in the direction of the lounge and assured him that he'd have Mickey stop before he went home. Jeff took a chair at a table where he could see everyone who came and left. He closely examined every man who could possibly be in his forties. No one seemed to match the physical description that his mother had given him.

Five minutes passed. . .then ten. . .fifteen and then twenty. Just when Jeff was getting ready to leave, a dark-haired man with graying temples approached him. "Hello, my name is Mickey Kilmer," he said as he extended his calloused hand. "I understand you were waiting to meet me."

Jeff stood and took the stranger's hand. He was amazed at

how much he physically resembled the older man. "I was trying to locate the Mickey Kilmer that used to live in Elders Point, Montana, more than twenty years ago. Could you possibly be he?"

The man's face reddened and the veins protruded from his neck. "What do you want him for?" he snapped.

Jeff gulped. "When he was a teenager he dated Beth Slater, and she later had a child."

"So what business is that of yours?" Mickey retorted.

"I am that child," Jeff replied meekly. "I'm in need of my medical history and was hoping to find some answers."

Mickey's hardened face twitched. "Sit down," he ordered. "I'll give you my basic medical history and that is all. I don't want anyone digging into my personal past. In fact, I'll contact my doctor, and have him mail you the entire file. Would that be enough to make you happy?" he added sarcastically.

In spite of Mickey's gruffness, Jeff beamed. "I'd appreciate that very much. There is a young woman I'm interested in marrying and having a family with, but I'm afraid to make any commitment until I'm certain I'm not the carrier of any genetic disorders."

At his words, Jeff studied the inner turmoil that reflected in his father's eyes. He wondered what he must have felt like having to sign over all rights to his son to another man. As hard as it was for him to make child support payments while he was in high school, Jeff was grateful that he had continued to maintain contact with his daughter. Charity had brought so much joy and meaning into his life during the past three years.

Finally, Mickey broke the silence. "As far as I know, I'm genetically normal. I've just done some stupid things in my life." He again hesitated, as if trying to make sense of what was happening to him. Then Mickey softened and his shoulders relaxed. "Jeff, do you remember going to Canada when you were four years old?"

"That was one of my earliest memories," Jeff replied, trying to recall the scene. "I loved that black sports car. I was so excited to get a chance to ride in it, but I didn't understand why I couldn't go back to my momma when it started to get dark."

"Taking you that day was one of the dumbest things I've ever done," Mickey confessed. "You could never understand what it's like to father a child and want to be a part of his life on the one hand and yet, at the same time, not want to assume the full responsibility of being a parent."

The wall between father and son was beginning to crumble, as Jeff understood the reason for the rejection by his biological father. "I identify with the situation more than you can imagine," Jeff replied. "During my senior year in high school, I, too, fathered a child. Sadly, our little Charity was born with severe spina bifida and hydrocephalus. I accepted paternity and have paid child support ever since. However, now that I'm finding myself falling in love with Charity's mother, I'm afraid to marry her for fear I was the cause of Charity's birth defects and any other children I might have would be affected."

Mickey put his hand on Jeff's shoulder. "You were much more of a man than I ever was under similar circumstances," he said. "I want to ask you just one question—would you still marry this girl if it could be proven that the birth defects without a shadow of a doubt came from the mother's side?"

Without hesitating, Jeff replied, "Of course I would. We would seek medical advice and trust God to direct our path as to family planning, adoption, or remaining childless. Aside from Charity, I mean."

"I think you answered your own question," Mickey replied

wisely. "Go ahead and date that girl. She'll be a mighty lucky woman to get you. In the meantime, I'll mail you my medical records." Mickey's eyes became distant. "Maybe we should get better acquainted. I think we have a lot to learn from each other."

eleven

"Sarah, why do you keep stealing my things?" Rebecca screamed. "I don't like living with a thief. I want you to leave immediately."

Sarah gulped. "Rebecca what are you looking for?" she asked calmly.

"I'm looking for my red afghan. It's my favorite one and it's not on my bed. You should go to jail for this," Rebecca retorted as she reached to grabbed Sarah's arm.

Sarah tried to remain calm, as her heart raced wildly. "I just finished washing the afghan. It's in the dryer now," she explained as she hurried to the basement, hoping the dryer had finished its cycle. She threw open the door, snatched the red afghan and rushed upstairs.

"My afghan. My afghan," Rebecca cried as she clutched it to her bosom. "I knew I would find it."

Sarah shrugged her shoulders. After two months of following a rigid routine caring for Rebecca while watching her slow yet steady decline, Sarah was able to find strength and encouragement from her faith in God and from her fellow Christians. As the external circumstances became more and more glum, Sarah's inner spirit grew vibrant. Even the people close to her began to notice the difference.

One morning on her way to class a familiar voice called out to her, Sarah turned and found herself face-to-face with Vanessa. "Sarah, how's it going? I haven't seen you in a long time." her former roommate exclaimed as she gave Sarah a quick hug.

"I've been keeping busy helping Rebecca, so I don't get out very often," Sarah replied as she studied the deep circles under Vanessa's eyes. "How are things going with you?"

Vanessa shook her head as they trudged toward Briar Hall. "I wish I could say great, but that would be the farthest from the truth. . . . I don't want to bore you with the gloomy details."

"Of course, I want to know the details," Sarah retorted. "I'm just sorry we haven't had so much time to spend together as when we shared the same dormitory room."

"Things have been pretty bad lately," Vanessa sighed, unable to hide her dejection.

Sarah was accustomed to Vanessa's mood swings, but this time it appeared more serious. "We've got to get together and talk, just like we used to," Sarah insisted. "Rebecca is generally in bed by eight thirty. Why don't you come over then and I'll make popcorn for the two of us?"

Vanessa beamed. "I'd like that," she replied. "You're one of the few people whom I feel comfortable talking with. We've been through a lot of rough times together."

With that, the two women bade each other good-bye and hurried to their separate classes. While waiting for her instructor to arrive, Sarah thought about the conversation that she just had. *Vanessa has often poured out her troubles to me,* she thought, *but I usually didn't pay much attention. At the time, it all seemed so trivial. Vanessa usually didn't take life too seriously, but this morning she appeared almost panicky. I wonder what's going on.*

After class, Sarah met Ryder in the Commons for their usual half hour of relaxation. "You never would have believed what happened last night with Rebecca," Sarah said softly.

"I'm almost afraid to ask," Ryder said cautiously.

"She screamed at me about stealing her red afghan and ordered me to leave. When I brought it up from the dryer, she said she knew all along that she would find it."

Ryder couldn't help but smile with sympathy for Sarah's frustrations. "I don't know how long you're going to be able care for Rebecca. It sounds like she's soon going to need more specialized care."

"I just take one day at a time," Sarah said before turning the conversation to her former roommate. "Ryder," she began as she admired his dark eyes and shining black hair. "Have you seen Vanessa much this semester?"

"Not really," he replied as he set his coffee cup into its saucer. "But I have heard that she was pretty upset when her boyfriend broke up with her. I have one class with her, and from what I can tell, she's starting to let her grades drop. She's also talking about going to the University of Iowa next year, but if she lets her G.P.A. fall, she won't be able to transfer her credits. Why do you ask?"

"I've been so wrapped up in my own problems, that I haven't kept in close contact with her," Sarah explained. "However, I ran into her between classes, and she sounded as if she was sinking into deep depression. I hadn't heard about her last breakup, but she's going to come over to Rebecca's tonight so we can talk."

Ryder wrinkled his forehead. "Good luck," he replied. "Those kinds of discussions can get pretty heavy at times."

"I know," Sarah sighed. "I'll need your prayer support."

"You can be assured of that," Ryder replied.

❧

That evening while Sarah helped prepare Rebecca for bed, her mind kept drifting back to the days when she lived in the dormitory. She had been extremely careful not to let anyone know her secret of having a disabled child at Little Lambs, and yet there had been such a change that came about in her life after she turned to God for help and opened up to those around her. In retrospect, she felt she had missed many opportunities to share the love and forgiveness of Jesus Christ that were available to all who believed. She was determined that if she had such an opportunity this evening with Vanessa she would not let it pass by again.

Promptly at 8:30, Vanessa rang the doorbell at Rebecca Hatfield's home. Sarah immediately answered the door and led her to the living room. Vanessa flopped onto the sofa. "Sarah, I don't know how you do it?" she exclaimed. "You've had ten times more problems in your life, and yet you always seem so in control and at peace. How do you do it? My life is falling apart; my boyfriend, Doug, left me for one of the cheerleaders and I have nothing left to look forward to."

The moment Sarah had been praying for was upon her. She was now able to share the faith and peace she had found in Jesus Christ. The two young women talked until 11:00 PM. Never before had they shared their innermost thoughts and fears. Not only did Vanessa tell of her broken romance but also of the emptiness and lack of purpose she felt. She admitted that she'd been hiding this void under a mask of parties and good times, but when her boyfriend left her, all the parties seemed pointless and there was nothing there to sustain her.

Sarah shared the source of her strength through her many trials and tribulations of life. She told about her pregnancy, being disowned by her mother, and, in the process, coming to know a love that never failed. She talked openly and freely about her relationship with Jesus. The more Vanessa heard, the more convinced she became that she wanted to learn more about the Savior that had helped Sarah through the difficult periods in her life.

"Vanessa, I don't know how I could possibly get through a hectic week without attending church and hearing Pastor Olson proclaim the gospel of Jesus Christ," Sarah stated firmly. "I'd like to share that source of strength with you. Would you like to come this Sunday?"

Much to Sarah's surprise, Vanessa replied, "I'd love to go, but I don't like to go someplace like that by myself."

"I wish I could go with you," Sarah smiled. "But I'm so busy getting Rebecca ready that I'm afraid I won't be able to help you. Give me until tomorrow, and I'll find someone to give you a ride and introduce you to those around you," she promised confidently.

After nearly two-and-a-half hours of intense conversation and soul-searching, Vanessa yawned. "Thanks for spending your entire evening with me. I feel so exhilarated. . .like I'm on the verge of an entirely new life. I'd better let you get some rest. We both have classes tomorrow."

Sarah rose to escort her friend to the door. "I'm so glad you came over. I'll call you tomorrow evening and finalize our plans for Sunday."

ও

The next day Sarah could scarcely wait for her few moments of relaxation in the Commons with Ryder. As soon as they were seated in their favorite booth she exclaimed, "Ryder, a very exciting thing happened last night. I was able to talk about spiritual things with Vanessa for the first time ever. She showed a lot of interest in the gospel and wants to attend church Sunday, if she doesn't have to go alone. Do you know anyone that might be willing to take her?"

Ryder smiled and reached for Sarah's hand. "If you wouldn't mind, I could give Vanessa a ride to church and introduce her to some of the others. I'm sure she'll feel right at home."

Sarah giggled. "Why would I mind?" she asked. "I was

just getting ready to ask you to take Vanessa."

"Sarah, you mean so much to me that I don't want to do anything that would cause you to be uncomfortable," Ryder explained. "I feel honored that you would consider having me give your old roommate a ride. Try to save us a seat close to you and Rebecca, so we can all be together."

That evening after Rebecca was in bed and the house was quiet, Sarah contemplated the events of the night before. She was excited about Vanessa's wanting to know more about the Christian faith and wanting to attend church, but, even though she tried to convince herself that Ryder's taking Vanessa to church didn't matter, Sarah knew it did. Why am I letting this bother me so much? She scolded herself. I have no long-term commitment to Ryder. Anyway, he'll be leaving in a few months for the University of Iowa.

❧

After a week of intense physical therapy, Jeff was able to put away his walker and walk confidently with a cane. The evening before he was to leave Spokane, he agreed to meet Mickey Kilmer for dinner. The young man was ecstatic when Mickey promised to bring copies of as many of his medical records as he could. His search was now over and he could become more serious with Sarah. It should have given him a sense of fulfillment, but something still seemed to be lacking. As evening approached, he realized that he wanted to continue his relationship with Mickey. More importantly, Jeff wanted to be sure that his biological father knew about the saving power of Jesus Christ.

Having a couple of hours to spare, Jeff stopped at the hospital gift shop and browsed through the books. There in the far back of the rack was a New Testament. Jeff admired its large, easy-to-read print and colorful cover. He held it in his hand while he continued browsing. Two rows lower was the book

How to Accept the Love and Forgiveness of Jesus Christ.

This'll be perfect, Jeff thought, *I know what I believe, but I often have trouble articulating my faith. These books say it so much better than I ever could.* He took his selections to the cashier and laid a twenty-dollar bill on the counter. The money seemed like such a small sacrifice to help introduce his natural father to the faith that he'd taken for granted all his life.

That evening the dinner conversation between the two men was more relaxed than either thought possible. Mickey openly shared the details of his struggle with drugs, his time in prison, and the months he had spent in rehabilitation as if this was the first time anyone had been concerned enough about him to listen.

"After I got out of prison, I was fortunate to get a job in the maintenance department of the Spokane Medical Clinic," Mickey explained. "It gave me a reason to stay drug and alcohol free these last few years." He then hesitated as a pained expression crossed his face. "In spite of all my determination and victories in overcoming my troubled background, I still feel an emptiness and lack of purpose."

Jeff was hoping for this opening. "Mickey, there's something that can fill that emptiness," he began. "The answer is in these books," he said as he took out the books he had purchased in the hospital gift shop. "These tell about the love and forgiveness in Christ so much better than I ever could. I don't know where I would be today without the strength of Jesus Christ and I'm certain He'll fill the same need for you."

Mickey looked at him skeptically. "I've tried everything else except religion and none of them seemed to work, so I might as well give it a try."

"This is more than just religion," Jeff protested, "I'm talking about a personal relationship with Jesus Christ and a belief that He has the power to forgive us our sins and give us eternal life."

Mickey thought for a moment, as if not completely understanding the difference between the two, but not wanting to go any deeper into the subject. Finally, he shrugged his shoulders, "Okay, I'll check it out for a few weeks. I don't have anything to lose."

"You'll never regret it," Jeff replied.

Mickey shrugged his shoulders. "By the way, did you watch this last Super Bowl game? Wasn't that a real barn burner?"

Picking up the cue, Jeff whispered a silent prayer for Mickey's spiritual quest and enjoyed their relaxed conversation for the remainder of the evening. Before they parted, the two men exchanged telephone numbers and addresses and promised to keep in contact.

Jeff's spirits were high when he returned to his motel room. His reason for keeping his distance from Sarah was now gone. He felt free to pursue a deeper relationship with her and see where it led. He took a scrap of paper from his wallet and dialed the number scribbled on it. He waited a few moments as he listened to the phone ring on the other end. Just when he was ready to hang up, a familiar voice entered the line.

"Hello. Rebecca Hatfield residence. Sarah Brown speaking."

"Hello, Sarah. This is Jeff. It's been a long time since I've talked with you," the young man began. "I've been extremely busy trying to catch up on my schoolwork and then I've spent the last few days in Spokane having physical therapy. I just wanted to let you know how much I've missed you."

"I wondered how you were doing," Sarah replied, sounding surprised by the unexpected telephone call. "I was beginning to wonder if I'd done something to upset you."

Jeff's heart sank. He hadn't meant to hurt her. "Of course

you didn't upset me. I would have let you know if you had. I'm the kind who'd rather talk things out than hold grudges," he assured her. "There was a reason for my preoccupation that I'd like to explain to you."

Sarah wrinkled her forehead. "You don't have to explain," she replied. "We both have busy lives right now and a lot to accomplish in a short amount of time."

"Sarah, it's more than that," Jeff persisted. "I won't be able to come to Rocky Bluff until spring break at the end of March, but I just want you to know how much I'm looking forward to seeing you then."

Sarah smiled. "I'm looking forward to seeing you too. Charity has often asked about you. She still talks about the time we took her to the mall over Thanksgiving."

"Memories of that day in the mall were what kept me going through those painful hours in the hospital," Jeff replied. "How is she doing? I imagine she's grown a lot since then."

Sarah shook her head. "Physically she's not growing so much as we'd like and she's well below normal for her age, but intellectually she seems to be well above average."

When the two finished discussing their daughter, the conversation changed to some of the frustrations involved in caring for someone with Alzheimer's. While Ryder was extremely intense and analytical about the problems that surrounded her, Sarah found Jeff's sense of humor and optimistic approach a welcome relief to the tension she bore.

After nearly an hour on the phone, Sarah reminded him, "We're running a pretty big phone bill and I haven't heard Rebecca for some while. I'd better check to make sure she is okay."

"It's been great talking with you," Jeff replied. "From now on I promise to call at least every three days and to e-mail you every day."

Sarah's spirits soared as she returned the phone to its cradle. Their relationship was now lifted to an even higher pitch.

ॐ

Sunday morning, Sarah helped Rebecca to her customary pew on the front left side of the church. Before the organist began, Vanessa slipped into the pew beside Sarah followed closely by Ryder. They all nodded in greeting just as the organist began the prelude. During the service, Sarah kept watching Vanessa from the corner of her eye. At times, she thought she saw tears glistening in the corners of her eyes and other times, when Pastor Olson talked about the love of God, Vanessa seemed to beam. There was no doubt in Sarah's mind that her former roommate was being touched by the entire worship experience.

Following the service, members and guests gathered for a time of fellowship in the multipurpose room next to the sanctuary. While Sarah helped Rebecca with her refreshments and found a comfortable seat in the corners so that they could enjoy watching the crowd, Ryder took Vanessa by the arm and introduced her to many in the assembly.

Sarah watched the happiness that radiated from Vanessa. She was not certain if it was the afterglow of a moving sermon, the warmth of the congregation. . .or. . .could it possibly be the attention she was receiving from Ryder.

"Hello, stranger," Teresa Olson, the pastor's wife, greeted as she took the chair next to Sarah. "I haven't talked with you in some time. How has it been going?"

"Really well, thank you," Sarah answered mechanically, but her eyes divulged the frustrations she was trying to mask.

"I have something I'd like to discuss with you in private. Would you mind joining me in the kitchen?" Teresa asked as she stood and motioned Sarah to follow. "Mrs. Fargo will be here to keep an eye on Rebecca for you."

Sarah and Teresa made themselves comfortable on a couple of stools in the far corner of the kitchen, away from the women who were serving the refreshments. "Now tell me the truth," Teresa stated firmly. "I realize that Rebecca is becoming more and more temperamental and unpredictable; is it beginning to bother you?"

Sarah gulped as tears built in her eyes. "How did you know? Is it that obvious?"

Teresa put her arms around Sarah. "I'm afraid so. Those dark bags under your eyes speak volumes."

"But. . .but. . .I don't want people to think I can't do my job," Sarah protested. "I really love Rebecca. Usually she's sweet to be around, but more and more, she's getting angry at little things and saying extremely demeaning things to me. I know she can't control everything she does, but that doesn't take away the sting."

"Sarah, you have a good understanding of what's going on, but unfortunately there will come a day when Rebecca will no longer be able to stay in her own home," Teresa reminded her. "Maybe that day is quickly approaching."

"But if I lose my job I won't be able to stay in school," Sarah blurted as her world seemed to come crashing in around her.

Teresa squeezed her hand. "Don't worry, we're not going to put you out in the street. Since there's a waiting list to get into the local care center, it would probably be wise if we put Rebecca's name on the waiting list now, so she'll be sure to have a place to go when her problems become too complex to be handled at home."

"I don't know what to say," Sarah responded as she took a tissue from her purse and dried her eyes.

"You don't have to say anything right now," Teresa tried to comfort her. "I just want you to remember you're not alone. The women that stay with her in the daytime face the same frustrations you do. If Rebecca ends up going to the care center before the semester is over, you can stay in the guest room in the parsonage for a few weeks."

"Thanks. I appreciate your understanding," Sarah replied and then glanced at her watch, "but now I suppose I'd better get Rebecca home so I can fix lunch for her. If she gets off schedule she can become extremely confused."

That afternoon while Rebecca was taking her afternoon nap, Sarah took out her computer applications textbook and began studying. There rarely seemed to be a break to lighten the intensity of her cycle—study. . .work. . .and visit her daughter. After she had read only five pages, the telephone rang.

"Hello, Rebecca Hatfield residence," she greeted.

"Hello, Sarah," Jeff replied. "I was just sitting here getting bored with my studies and wondering what you were doing."

Sarah giggled. "I'm doing the same thing—just sitting here getting bored with my studies."

"I wish I were there to help enjoy your boredom," Jeff replied, "but I'll have to wait three more weeks. How has little Charity been?"

"She's doing great," Sarah replied, "but she's definitely developing an extremely strong will. Yesterday, she had to spend ten minutes in "time out" for scratching one of the other children for playing with the same ball she wanted to play with."

"I guess it's all part of learning to get along with others," Jeff replied with a chuckle.

For the next fifteen minutes, the pair discussed the antics of their daughter as if they were a normal married couple, instead of two college students trying to make the best of the consequences of the sins of their youth.

When they finally ended their conversation and Sarah

hung up the phone, a feeling of hope and optimism overtook her. After her talk with Teresa and hearing Jeff's concern for Charity, Sarah began considering the possibilities of what might happen to herself when Rebecca went to the nursing home. Life might have been difficult at times, but there always seemed to be someone who stepped in to help her carry her burdens.

twelve

Sarah hurried to the booth she and Ryder usually shared in the Commons after class each day. She was anxious to learn of Vanessa's reaction to the church service and hoped that she would be interested in attending on a regular basis. Had Ryder been able to help her understand the basis of faith in Jesus Christ? When Sarah arrived, she found Ryder already in the booth with a soft drink waiting for her.

"Hi," he greeted jovially. "What took you so long?"

Sarah glanced at her watch and smiled. She was actually five minutes earlier than normal. "I just can't run as fast as I used to," she retorted as she slipped into the booth across from her classmate. "I could hardly wait to see you. Vanessa looked as if she was extremely moved during the worship service. What did she say afterwards?"

"I took her out to lunch, and we had a very interesting conversation," Ryder explained, unable to hide his excitement. "To make a long story short, she ended up saying that she did believe in Jesus Christ as her Savior and was interested in learning more. I told her about the class for new believers and she seemed eager to attend it."

"I'm not surprised," Sarah replied. "Even when Vanessa appeared to be only interested in superficial things, underneath there was a sensitive longing, waiting to be tapped. I'm sure she'll take on her spiritual quest with the same intensity she does the rest of life."

Ryder studied the deep creases on Sarah's forehead. "How have things been going with Rebecca?" he queried.

Sarah shook her head. "Each day is worse than the day before. Some days I'm beginning to question my own sanity. After listening to Rebecca talk, I require a good reality check."

"I know it's tough," Ryder replied, "but it will all be over in a few weeks."

"That's the only thing that keeps me going," Sarah sighed and then took a deep breath as if to refresh her entire being.

The pair continued sharing news of their church, their class work, activities at Little Lambs; however, Ryder appeared more distracted than normal. Finally, he reached across the table and took Sarah's hand. "You have so many pressures on you at this time, that I've hesitated to add to it," he began, "but I have some good news and some bad news to tell you."

Sarah set her can of soda on the table and leaned forward. "Give the good news first. I need some cheering up."

"I got a part-time job as an assistant in the pediatrics ward in the hospital," he explained. "They heard about my work at Little Lambs and approached me about providing entertainment for the sick children for a couple of hours every afternoon. It sounds like it would be a lot of fun and would also be good experience for me."

Sarah smiled and reached across the table and took his hand. "Congratulations. When do you begin?"

"That's the bad news. I start tomorrow, and we won't be able to meet anymore after classes," Ryder replied. "I've enjoyed our times together, and I'm going to miss our regular, heart-to-heart talks. They've been the highlight of my day."

"I will too," Sarah admitted, trying to hide her disappointment. "I don't know how I could have survived the last few weeks if it hadn't been for these few minutes we've had together each day."

"Don't worry. I'm not abandoning you," Ryder assured her as he squeezed her hand. "I'll try to call you every night and see how your day went. It's not so good as face-to-face, but it beats trying to go it alone like you did when you first moved in with Rebecca."

"I'd appreciate that," she replied, realizing that with Jeff's calling long distance every other evening, there could potentially be a time conflict. She was grateful that Rebecca had call waiting on her telephone.

As the two finished their drinks, Ryder glanced at his watch. "We'd better get moving if you're going to get to Little Lambs by three o'clock. There's no shuttle today, but I'll run and get my car and pick you up at the south entryway."

"Thanks," Sarah replied. "I forgot all about the schedule change. You always seem to be available when I need help."

≥

When Sarah arrived at Little Lambs, Charity was just waking from her nap. She hugged her daughter close to her bosom and then carried her into the playroom. This time Charity was anxious to play on the floor with a little boy about her own age, giving Sarah a chance to talk with Dawn. For the last several days, Charity had monopolized all of Sarah's time while she was at Little Lambs so she had little time for even minor discussions with anyone else.

"How has Rebecca been lately?" Dawn queried. "When I saw her in church Sunday, she didn't look well."

Sarah shook her head. "She's due for a physical next week, but her temperament is becoming extremely difficult to deal with. She's doing more and more shouting and is starting to take swings at me when she doesn't get her way."

"That sounds serious," Dawn replied as the furrow in her forehead deepened. "Have you told anyone yet about this behavior?"

Sarah took a deep breath. Although she knew Rebecca's change of behavior was caused by the natural progression of the disease, somehow she was afraid that people would think that she couldn't do her job properly. After all, she had learned to care for extremely disabled children, why couldn't she also care for mentally disabled elderly people. "I talked to Teresa after church Sunday, and she thought they needed to get Rebecca's name on the waiting list of the care center," she explained cautiously. "However, what I'm concerned about is that she'll have to go to the nursing home before I'm finished with college and I won't have a job, nor a place to stay."

"I don't think you'll have to worry about that," Dawn assured her. "We have a small room in the back that is being used for storage right now. If push comes to shove, we can clean that out for you and you can earn your room and board by taking care of the children several hours each day. We've found ourselves short of staff in the evenings when we're trying to get the children to bed."

Sarah relaxed. She now had two offers for housing. "That seems like an ideal backup plan," she replied. "That will give me more time to learn to care for disabled children and at the same time I can send out résumés and begin looking for a full-time job."

Just then, a unified cry erupted from the floor as Charity and her playmate each tried to claim possession of the same toy bear at the same time. Sarah grabbed Raggedy Ann and offered it to Charity who immediately claimed it and forgot about the stuffed toy they were fussing over. The rest of the time with Charity flew by, and before she realized it, the time had come to hug her daughter good-bye and go care for Rebecca. Each time she found it harder and harder to leave her daughter, but if she was to accomplish her final goal, she had to make the sacrifice.

❧

Jeff Blair clenched the steering wheel as his car made the

hairpin turns over Rodger's Pass. It had been more than four months since his fateful accident, but as he approached the site, it became more and more difficult for him not to turn around in terror and return to Missoula. His hands were sweating and his breathing increased. He prayed for strength to overcome his fears and focused his mind on little Charity and Sarah. He realized that if he did not overcome his anxiety of driving mountain passes he would always be separated from the woman he was growing to love.

Once he had passed the exact location of the accident, a sense of relief overwhelmed him. He breathed a big sigh and smiled at himself in the rearview mirror. He had faced one of the biggest fears in his life and, with God's help, had overcome it. Jeff now felt the courage to take on any other challenge that might present itself.

Upon arriving in Rocky Bluff, Jeff went directly to Little Lambs and rang the doorbell. "Jeff, it's good to see you again," Dawn greeted as she motioned him to enter. "How have you been doing?"

Jeff entered the hallway and laid his cane against the wall while he removed his coat. "It was a long, difficult trip," he admitted, "but I finally made it."

Dawn studied the young man's face. He looked as if he'd aged five years since she had last seen him in the hospital in Great Falls after Charity's seizure at the end of November. "Charity is still sleeping," she began. "Why don't you come into the family lounge with me. We have a lot of catching up to do."

Jeff hung his coat on the rack, took a spot on the end of the sofa, and laid the cane beside him. After sitting in the same position for nearly four hours during the drive, the muscles in his back and legs were beginning to throb, but he tried to keep his face from reflecting his pain. "How has Charity been?" he asked as Dawn took a seat in the chair beside him.

"She's been doing remarkably well," Dawn assured him. "You'll be surprised by how much she's grown since the last time you saw her."

"Sarah mentioned over the phone that she's had more seizures since the bad one in November. How serious have they been?" Jeff queried.

Dawn smiled as she tried to choose the right words to explain Charity's condition. "Of course, no seizure is good for the body, but from what we can tell, they have all been minor and there have not been any lasting effects. So far, the doctor hasn't prescribed any seizure medication."

"That takes a load off my mind," Jeff sighed. "Seizures can be really scary for me."

Dawn eyed the cane beside the young man. "How have you been doing?" she asked with concern. "Have you been mending well from the accident?"

Jeff thought back through the months of agony and physical therapy. At times, he wasn't sure if he'd ever walk again, but his strong determination had carried him over the difficult spots. "I'm getting along fairly well," he replied. "I'm not ready to run the Boston Marathon, by any means, but I've come a long way. I've had to accept the fact that my football career is over, and I'm changing my major from physical education to business administration."

"I'm sure you'll have a good future in whatever you choose to do," Dawn assured him. "Are you still having a lot of trouble getting around?"

"Sometimes," Jeff admitted, knowing there was no way he could hide the depth of his problem from the trained nurse. "When it's icy out, or if I'm extremely tired, I still need the walker. However, I feel very self-conscious when I have the walker. Everyone assumes that walkers are for old people and they seemed shocked seeing a former jock shuffling along with one."

"I'm sure, if there are stares, they're in sympathy and not shock," Dawn replied and then felt it wiser to change the subject. "I'm sorry I haven't been able to get hold of Stuart Leonard yet to help you locate your birth father."

Before Jeff could respond, the doorbell rang and Dawn hurried to answer it. Upon hearing Sarah's voice, Jeff picked up his cane and ambled to the hallway to greet her. Oblivious to the director standing in the corner, they gave each other a fond embrace and a short kiss.

Sarah was shocked to see how much weight Jeff had lost, but she tried her best to mask it. "How was your trip?" she asked as Jeff took her hand and led her to the sofa in the lounge while Dawn quietly slipped away to the playroom so the two could be alone.

Jeff shook his head. "It was extremely long and tiresome," he replied. "If I didn't know that you and Charity were on the other side of the mountain, I don't think I could have made it."

"Flattery will get you everywhere," Sarah giggled. "I have to admit that it's good seeing you again. It seems like it was a lifetime ago since we last saw each other."

"To me, it seems like ten lifetimes," Jeff replied just as a familiar cry came from the children's bedroom.

Sarah hurried to get her daughter while Jeff shuffled slowly behind, bearing part of his weight on his cane. By the time Jeff had gotten to the bedroom door, Sarah was already returning with her daughter in her arms. Charity's eyes brightened. "Daddy," she squealed as she reached out for her father to take her.

Suddenly the truth of his injuries bore down on him. He would not be able to carry his daughter and walk with his cane at the same time. Sensing what was going through Jeff's head, Sarah said, "Charity, let's go to the playroom and then Daddy will hold you."

When Jeff was seated comfortably in one of the rocking chairs, Sarah placed their daughter on his lap. He tried not to grimace with pain as she wiggled against his tender muscles. "Hi, Daddy," she said as she held tightly to his hand. "I missed you."

"I missed you, too, Muffin," he replied. "You've gotten so big and so pretty since I last saw you."

"Play on the floor, play on the floor," she pled as a pained expression crossed Jeff's face.

Sarah quickly said, "Daddy hurts too much to get on the floor. I'll get you your favorite storybook and Daddy can read to you."

After Jeff finished reading the story to his daughter, Sarah put her in her wheelchair and slid the tray into place. With Charity in her chair, Jeff was able to help her color and play with her toys on the tray. When they tired of the toys, Jeff tried to teach her to sing "Jesus Loves Me."

Charity quickly learned the words and tune to the song. When Jeff sang, "little Ones to Him belong, they are weak, but He is strong," his eyes met Sarah's. "After playing super jock for so many years, after my accident I once again learned what it felt like to be weak, and know that Jesus is the only one who is strong."

Time passed swiftly as the three tried to accept Jeff's new limitations and discover ways to modify the simple routines they were accustomed to. At quarter until five, Sarah reluctantly said, "I hate to leave, but I have to fix dinner for Rebecca."

"It's nearly time for the children to begin getting ready for dinner," Jeff noted. "I still need to get a motel room for the evening so I'd better be going as well. Would you mind if I came over to Rebecca's later this evening to see you?"

Sarah smiled as she took their child from Jeff's lap, hugged her, and then placed her on the mat in the center of the room where Dawn was playing with two other children. The pair walked slowly to the lounge to get their coats. "I'd love to have you come this evening," Sarah said. "Rebecca is usually in bed by eight-thirty. I could fix us some treats and we can catch up on the last few months. So much has happened since we've last been together."

❧

As Sarah went about her nightly routine of feeding Rebecca and preparing her for bed, her mind drifted back to the short time she had with Jeff that afternoon. Even though most of their attention was centered on Charity, there were times that personal glances intensified her need to find answers to unasked questions. Jeff had obviously changed. Even though his sense of humor was still intact, there was seriousness about him that she had not seen before. She could hardly wait for him to arrive later that evening.

❧

Likewise, Jeff could hardly wait to spend time alone with Sarah. He drove to the Round Rock Motel and checked in, then crossed the street to the Green House Family Restaurant. He noticed something different about Sarah. She appeared tired and worn, yet, at the same time, excited to see him. In just a few hours, he would be able to share some of the innermost thoughts with her that had been building for the last four months.

Promptly at 8:30 Jeff rang the doorbell to Rebecca Hatfield's home. He waited for what seemed an eternity before Sarah appeared. "I'm sorry it took so long," she greeted as she motioned Jeff to enter. "I was busy making a special dessert for you and my hands were all messy."

Jeff leaned over and gave her a quick kiss. "You shouldn't have gone to any extra trouble. Just having time to be alone together is enough to make me happy."

In spite of Jeff's mild protests to Sarah's extra work, he thoroughly enjoyed the apple crisps and whipped cream she set before him. As they exchanged the details of the difficulties they each had faced during the last few months, the bond between them intensified. After they finished their first cup of coffee, Jeff took Sarah's hand. "I'm sorry I stayed so aloof for several months, but I had a lot of things going on in my mind that I had to work out before I felt I could pursue our relationship."

Sarah wrinkled her forehead in anticipation of what he had to say. She felt certain that, whatever the reason for his distance, she could easily forgive him.

"Sarah," he began softly, "as I lay in the hospital, staring at the blank ceiling hour after hour, all I could think about was you. I knew that what we did years ago was wrong, and I wondered if I might have been the cause of Charity's birth defects. Perhaps I carried some defective genes. I didn't want to become close to anybody until I knew my medical history."

"Did you ever find your natural father?" Sarah asked, as she thought about her own father whom she had seen only twice since she was three. A few years ago, she learned of his death from AIDS.

"I met him in Spokane while I was there for therapy," Jeff began. "He gave me full access to his medical records and there was nothing remarkable about them, just normal illnesses. Since I now know that I'm not carrying some sort of bad gene, I feel free to pursue a normal male/female relationship and enter the dating arena. However, you're the only one whom I've ever held a deep fondness for."

Sarah held Jeff's hand and gazed into his soft green eyes. "I can understand why you might worry about carrying a bad gene since you didn't know your natural father, but don't you realize that I've lain awake at nights worrying about the same thing? That I was the reason for Charity's problems."

Jeff had never before questioned Sarah about her father. He had always assumed it was something that was too painful for her to discuss and did not want to intrude into her private thoughts, until now. "What happened to your father? Do you know anything about his medical history?"

Sarah took a deep breath. "My parents divorced when I was small and I never really knew my father. Mother never spoke kindly of him and was not sure of his medical background, so when Charity was born with a birth defect I often wondered if I was carrying a bad gene. Dawn tried to convince me that no one knows what causes spina bifida, but doctors are suspicious that it's the lack of folic acid in the mother's body. Either way, I felt that I was either carrying a bad gene or something was lacking in my body to cause the defect, so I vowed I would never marry. I did not want another child to suffer the things Charity has suffered."

"But God has a purpose for Charity," Jeff persisted. "She was not a horrible accident." Jeff paused. The two sat in silence for several minutes before he continued, "We both suffered needlessly by blaming ourselves for Charity's birth defects. If we would have trusted God's wisdom and accepted the path He set before us, we could have spared ourselves so much heartache. . . . Sarah, you mean so much to me. I hope our lives will grow in the same direction so that someday we might become one."

thirteen

Sarah Brown perused the bulletin board outside the college placement service office. It had been a long, uphill struggle, but she was now within two months of graduation. She had already accepted the fact that there were few jobs in her field in Rocky Bluff and that she'd have to consider some of the bigger cities of Montana. She thought about returning to Billings, so her mother could help her with Charity. However, if she had little Charity with her in Billings, Jeff would not be able to be an active part of her life. Suddenly, a poster caught her eye.

Job Fair
All Careers
Memorial Union Building
University of Montana Campus
Missoula, Montana
May 5th
9:00–3:00

I sure would like to go to that, Sarah pondered. *I've always liked Missoula and it's growing so fast that I'm sure there are plenty of job opportunities. If I raise Charity in Missoula, she'll at least have a chance to know her father. But it's not likely that I'd be able to get enough money for the bus and a motel room. Even if I did get a job there, I wouldn't have the money to move there and support myself until I got my first paycheck.*

In spite of her doubts, Sarah jotted the date of the job fair on a scrap of paper in her notebook and hurried on to class. All during the period, while the instructor droned on and occasionally paused to ask students questions, Sarah could not keep her mind off the possibility of getting a job in Missoula She tried to convince herself that her interest in Missoula was strictly for Charity's benefit, but deep inside she knew that she, too, would like to be close to Jeff Blair.

While Sarah was walking across campus to the bus stop, Ryder's familiar voice shouted, "Hey, Sarah. Wait up."

Sarah turned and waited for Ryder Long to catch up with her. It had been nearly two months since their daily meetings in the Commons had stopped when he took the part-time job at the hospital. They had shared greetings before and after classes and he did call occasionally in the evenings, but not every night as he'd promised. And she had noticed that he had been bringing Vanessa to church nearly every Sunday. It seemed as if their lives were taking them in different directions.

"Hi, Ryder," she greeted as he caught up with her. "How have you been doing?"

"I've been awfully busy," he replied as they continued walking toward the bus stop. "I've been putting in a lot more hours at the hospital, and I'm trying to get all A's this semester."

"A's shouldn't be too hard for you to get," Sarah teased.

"Ha! If you only knew how hard I have to work to get them," he joked back and then became serious. "It's paying off though. I just got word that I was accepted into the University of Iowa for next fall. I'm really excited about going," he paused and took a deep breath before continuing. "Vanessa White was also accepted there. I don't know if you've heard or not, but we have started going steady and things seem to be developing very quickly between the two of us."

Even though Sarah had been extremely fond of Ryder, she'd never felt anything more than friendship for him. He had been there to give her strength and encouragement during some extremely difficult times. They had shared a lot of laughs and good times, but he had always treated her more like a sister than a girlfriend. Yet, her heart dropped a little to have her suspicion confirmed. She thought she saw sparks between Ryder and Vanessa while they were in church. Little things, like how their eyes met or holding hands under the hymnal, betrayed that theirs was not just a casual relationship.

"I'm so happy for you," Sarah said, trying to act pleased. "You make a handsome couple and have a lot in common. I wish you the best."

"Thanks, and I hope things work out for you," Ryder replied. "You've been a true friend and a model student."

Just then, the shuttle to downtown arrived, and Sarah said good-bye as she stepped on board. Strange emotions enveloped her as the familiar houses flew past the window. Surely I'm not jealous, she scolded herself. Maybe I'll always have a soft spot in my heart for Ryder, because, outside of Jeff, he's the only guy that has ever paid any attention to me.

Charity was already up from her afternoon nap when Sarah arrived. As soon as she saw her mother enter the play-room, she immediately rolled her wheelchair across the room to meet her. "Hi, Mommy," she squealed.

"Hi, Sweetheart," her mother replied. "What are you doing?"

"We're playing with clay," the little girl announced. "See. . . I made a snake."

"That's a nice snake," Sarah replied. "Can you make some baby snakes to go with it?"

"Sure," Charity replied as she turned her interest back to the clay on the tray of her wheelchair.

Just then, Ryan and Dawn entered the room, each carrying a child. "Hi, Sarah. It's good to see you again," Ryan greeted as he and Dawn each took a rocking chair. "How have you been doing?"

Sarah sank into a chair beside Dawn. "I'm needing to start my job search for serious, but I don't know what to do. There aren't many jobs in my field here in Rocky Bluff, yet it's so complicated trying to apply for jobs in other towns."

"I know how that is," Ryan agreed. "I've been there myself. It's tough, but it can be done."

"There's a job fair in Missoula May fifth," Sarah explained. "I'd really like to go, but I don't have money for a bus ticket or a motel room."

Dawn and Ryan exchanged glances as if they were both thinking the same thing. "We have a medical seminar in Missoula the fourth and fifth. We could give you a ride," Dawn suggested. "I think several of the church campus ministries have guest rooms for student use. I could check around and see if one is available that weekend."

Sarah beamed. "Really? I can hardly believe it could be that easy."

"Don't worry," Dawn replied. "Applying for jobs and attending job fairs is hard work. It can almost be a full-time job in and of itself."

❧

Jeff Blair tapped on the door of his college advisor's office. It was two days before pre-registration for fall semester and Jeff had finally accepted the fact that he was not going to be able to major in physical education. His minor was in business administration, so now was the time to make an official change.

"Come in," the gray-haired professor shouted. "It's open."

Jeff timidly opened the door, his cane in hand. "Good day, sir."

"Have a seat young man," Doctor Westcott commanded. "What can I do to help?"

"I think I need to change my major," Jeff began cautiously. "I don't think I'll ever be so physically fit as I was before my car accident."

Doctor Westcott's expression softened. "I'm sorry to hear that," he replied, "but if you have to make a change, it's better to do it before you take any more credits that won't count toward graduation."

"That's what I figured," Jeff sighed. "That's why I need help in changing my major before I pre-register for fall classes."

Doctor Wescott reached for the current college catalog and then into the file beside his desk for Jeff's grade sheets. "What were you considering majoring in?" he asked.

"I was considering business administration," Jeff replied, "since that had been my minor and I already have had a couple of introductory classes."

"Sounds like a wise decision," Doctor Wescott replied. "Many students start out majoring in physical education and then change to majors not based on physical ability that will diminish in a few short years." The professor then spent the next fifteen minutes explaining which classes Jeff would need to complete a business major.

The more Dr. Wescott explained, the more excited Jeff became. "I've always liked math," he responded. "I should have picked this as a major early on, instead of wasting my time with physical education."

"A lot of students have to try several different majors, before they find one that suits them," the professor encouraged. "In fact, it's best to get as much training in a given field before you get close to graduation. Just yesterday, I had a local realtor contact me about arranging for a paid-intern program. Would you be interested in checking into it?"

Jeff beamed. "That would be perfect," he exclaimed. "Since I can't stand on my feet for a long period of time, I've had to give up my job at the Pizza Parlor. I was going to have to look for another job anyway."

Doctor Westcott picked up the phone and within minutes he had arranged for Jeff to interview with the Big Sky Realtors the following day. Jeff thanked his advisor for his help and left his office, the happiest he'd been since he'd found his natural father and learned that he wasn't a carrier of genetic defects.

☙

May fifth, dressed in a conservative plaid suit with a pale blue blouse, Sarah walked nervously into the Memorial Union Building at the University of Montana, carrying a folder filled with professional résumés. The room was full of rows and rows of booths with banners hanging over them, naming their particular business. Sarah walked slowly through the crowd of eager students, trying to locate those companies that were interested in hiring computer technicians.

After she had located ten such businesses at the fair, Sarah approached a young woman behind the table. "Hello," she greeted as she extended her right hand. "My name is Sarah Brown. I'll be receiving an associate's degree in computer technology from Rocky Bluff Community College. I'm seeking a computer technician position."

"You came to the right place," the businesswoman smiled, seeming genuinely interested in Sarah's background. Do you have copy of your résumé with you?"

Sarah handed the résumé to the woman who glanced over it and then motioned her to have a chair. After a brief conversation, the older woman gave Sarah a copy of the job description and her business card, and promised to be in touch.

At first, Sarah was encouraged, but as she listened to the conversations around her, she began to wonder how many others received the same treatment. Trying to mask her feeling of desperation, Sarah talked with every business that was looking for a computer technician. When she exhaustedly left the campus at the end of the afternoon, she mused, *I did the best I could in trying to obtain a job, now I've got to relax and let God direct my path. He knows just the right place for me.*

Sarah walked slowly across the street to the restaurant where Jeff had agreed to meet her after the job fair. He was sitting in the window watching, when he saw her approach. He limped out the door toward her. "Hi, Sarah. Did you have any luck?" he greeted as he put his arm around her and guided her into the restaurant.

"I hope so," she sighed. "I gave it my best shot. Several businesses seemed interested, but I won't know for several weeks. A few said they wanted to check my references and then get back to me."

"That's a good sign," Jeff exclaimed as he led the way to a corner booth. "Just think, in a couple of months you could be working in Missoula and we could see each other nearly every day."

"I hope so," Sarah replied as the waitress brought them their menus.

After they placed their order, Jeff took Sarah's hand, "I have more good news," he said. "I've changed my major to business administration and have just accepted a position as a paid intern at Big Sky Realty. In spite of my physical problems, I can now get back on track with a good career possibility."

Sarah's spirits soared as she thought of having Jeff close by to talk and laugh with every day. He was the one person who always seemed to understand the joys and frustrations that she felt, regardless of what was happening in his own life. She prayed that her desire for a job in Missoula, where she could be closer to the man she was growing to love, would not be in vain.

ಌ

The next day, on their return trip to Rocky Bluff with Ryan and Dawn, Sarah was anxious to share her response and hopes from the job fair and Jeff's good fortune in finding a job. "I want to get excited about the possibilities before me," Sarah explained, "but there are still so many loose ends that would have to work out in order for me to get a job and move to Missoula. I don't know where I could get the money to move and live on until I get my first paycheck."

"Don't give up hope," Ryan reminded her. "If you get a job, I'll go with you to the credit union and co-sign a short-term loan for you. You have a lot of friends in Rocky Bluff who are anxious to help you. You'll be surprised who'll come to your assistance."

Sarah's eyes widened. "I've never had a loan before," she exclaimed, then relaxed, and giggled. "I guess that will be my first step into the adult world."

"It happens to the best of us," Dawn teased before she became serious. "The important thing is to make your payments on time and establish a good credit rating."

"That's what worries me," Sarah replied. "I saw how hard my mother had to work to pay the rent, buy the food, and get all the bills paid each week. Now that I'm faced with the same challenges, I have a better appreciation for all she's done for me."

The day after Sarah returned to Rocky Bluff, she had trouble focusing on her classes. She was now within three weeks of graduation and it was becoming harder and harder to concentrate on her studies. During class time, she often caught herself staring out the window, imagining herself with little Charity in her own apartment in Missoula. She began to wonder how difficult it would be to find adequate day care for a disabled child, but she tried not to dwell on that obstacle until she had total custody of her daughter.

When Sarah returned to Rebecca's home that evening, Teresa Olson greeted her while Rebecca sat on the sofa, crying softly. "Come join us," Teresa called as Sarah unlocked the front door and hung her coat in the hall closet. "We have something to discuss with you."

A puzzled look covered Sarah's face while she took a seat on the sofa beside Rebecca. "What's happening?"

"I just received word that there is an opening at the care center and Rebecca can move in tomorrow," Teresa explained. "Rebecca is just getting used to the idea of having to leave her home. After dinner tonight, I was going to help her decide what she'd like to take with her."

Sarah faced the news with mixed emotions. Since Rebecca's personality was beginning to change and she was now taking swings at caregivers who did not do what she wanted them to do, Sarah knew the care center was the only solution. Yet, Rebecca loved her home. It seemed her last link to her former life, and it was now being taken away from her.

Sarah fixed dinner for Teresa and Rebecca while Teresa tried explaining some of the activities and services of the care center. One minute Rebecca seemed accepting of the idea and the next minute she would say, "That's nice, but I'm not going."

During dinner, Teresa tried to keep the conversation on the happy times in Rebecca's life, the years she was high school librarian in Rocky Bluff, the time she spent as librarian on Guam, and the years she was married to Andy Hatfield. Rebecca smiled with delight as she recalled those happy days. Yet the closer the stories got to the present the less Rebecca was able to relate to the situation.

After they had finished eating, Sarah began clearing the table while Teresa accompanied Rebecca into her bedroom and began going through Rebecca's things. Teresa helped Rebecca fill two suitcases and then helped her select her favorite pictures to take with her. At times Rebecca did not appear to understand why she was putting her favorite things in a suitcase, but Teresa tried to help her use her best judgment in the selections.

When the two suitcases and a cardboard box were full, Teresa helped Rebecca prepare for bed.

It was the last night she would be sleeping in her own home.

&

Sarah was wiping the counter when Teresa returned to the kitchen and took two coffee mugs from the cupboard. "Sarah, can I get a cup of coffee for you?"

"Sure," Sarah replied, trying to mask her unsettledness. "I was just finishing up."

Teresa filled both mugs, set them on the kitchen table, and motioned Sarah to take the chair beside her. "I'm certain you have a lot of questions about what is happening to Rebecca and how it will affect you."

Sarah grimaced. "You're right, I do," she replied cautiously. "I'm within three weeks of graduation. I'll not only need a place to stay, but I'll need cash to pay my living expenses. Dawn has offered me assistance if Rebecca went to a nursing home, but we haven't discussed it in detail yet."

"While you were in class today, I had a long discussion with Dawn and Ryan as to how best to help you make a transition into the workaday world," Teresa explained. "Rebecca's house will have to be put on the market, and it may take several weeks before it is sold. In the meantime, we thought it would be better if you kept on living here, both for security and to keep up the appearance of the house."

"Thank you," Sarah replied. "I really appreciate everything people are doing to help me. I don't know what I'd have done without that help."

"The important thing is that when you are on your feet, you turn around and help others in need," Teresa reminded her. She then took another sip of her coffee. "In the meantime, Sarah, Dawn agreed to pay you for four hours of work each day for at least a month. Do you think you could keep up with your schoolwork and work that much?"

Sarah's eyes became misty. "Like I said when I took this job caring for Rebecca, I'll do whatever is necessary to be able to finish college, get a job, and obtain full custody of my daughter."

fourteen

Sarah hung her coat in the closet of Rebecca's home, laid her books on the end table, and collapsed onto the sofa. It seemed strange returning to an empty house. Spending five hours a day on campus and then another four hours working at the Little Lambs Children's Center was exhausting, but worth the effort. It had been two weeks since Rebecca had moved to the care center and Sarah had just ten days until her graduation. Her mother and younger brother were going to drive from Billings for the ceremony, and Jeff was planning to come from Missoula. From that point on, the future was a misty fog. However, tonight she was too tired to worry about anything.

Just then, the telephone rang. Sarah mustered all the lagging energy she could and went to the kitchen and picked up the phone. "Hello," she greeted as she sank into a kitchen chair.

"Hello. Is Sarah Brown available, please?"

"This is she," Sarah replied, wondering who would be calling using such a businesslike tone.

"This is Eric Johnson from Quality Computer Center in Missoula. I met you in the job fair a couple of weeks ago and have since checked your references. If you're still available, I would like to offer you the position of computer technician at Quality Computers. Would you be interested?"

Sarah gasped. She remembered having talked with him, but felt she had little chance of getting the position. She had noticed a long line of applicants approach their booth since

Quality Computers was one of the largest computer stores in Missoula and offered the best salary package. "Yes. . .sure," she stammered.

"When will you be able to start?" Eric asked. "I realize that you'll need some time to relocate."

Sarah's heart raced. She'd waited for this moment for three years. But now that it was here, she was unsure of what to say. "I graduate a week from Saturday," she began hesitatingly. "I could start any time after that."

"You'll need some time to apartment hunt and get settled," the store manager noted. "Would you be able to start work on Monday, June fifth?"

"Sure," Sarah readily agreed. "What time would you like me there?"

"We open at nine o'clock. If you would come to my office then, we could begin filling out the paperwork," Eric said. "In the meantime, if there's anything we can do to help you relocate, please let us know."

A few minutes before, Sarah had felt totally exhausted, but now her adrenalin was pumping and she could scarcely control her excitement. "Thank you, thank you very much," she exclaimed. "I'll be there bright and early on the fifth of June."

As soon as she hung up, Sarah immediately dialed Jeff's home. Jeff seemed to be even more excited about Sarah's job offer than she was. "Not only did you get hired by the best computer store in Missoula," he exclaimed, "but Quality Computers is only two blocks from Big Sky Realtors where I'll be working."

"I can hardly believe it," Sarah replied. "I only have a couple of weeks to get things worked out. I don't know where to begin."

"God will direct you, the same way as He's done so many times before," Jeff tried to comfort her. "I'll start looking around for an apartment for you that'll be close to your work. The first of June is a good time to apartment hunt, since a lot of college students will be moving out and heading home for the summer."

"Thanks," Sarah replied. "Tomorrow when I'm in the computer lab, I'll go to the *Missoulian's* web site and check their classified section for rentals as well.

"Someday I'd like to have my own house," Sarah continued, but now I'd be happy with a simple one-bedroom furnished apartment."

Jeff smiled as he gazed out the windows to the distant mountains. "Someday I'd like to have a large house on acreage with horses. However, it would have to be on a main road and close enough to a city so that I could commute to work every day."

The young couple continued talking for almost an hour, both shared their hopes and dreams for their future. After knowing each other for nearly four years, their lives were now headed in the same direction. When Sarah finally hung up the telephone, she realized that it was much too late to call Dawn and Ryan and tell them the good news. With an early morning class, she wondered if she would be able to contain her excitement until she could talk with them when she went to work late in the afternoon.

Sarah could scarcely sleep that night as her mind continued to race in anticipation of her good fortune. She was up early, walked the three blocks to the bus stop, and arrived on campus as soon as the computer lab opened. She immediately went to the *Missoulian's* web page and printed out a list of ten possible apartments. She then went to an online street atlas and located them on the Missoula city map. Three of them were within walking distance to Quality Computers. All of this was done before she went to her first class.

Sarah eagerly told her entire political science class about

her exciting job offer. "Congratulations," Ryder said as the others nodded in agreement. "I knew you could do it."

As soon as classes were over, Sarah hurried to the bus stop. The warm spring breeze invigorated her. As she waited, she began to do her mental calculations. From the prices she saw in the Missoula newspaper, she got the general idea of the amount she'd need for a deposit and first month's rent on an apartment. She estimated the amount of money she'd need for groceries and incidentals until she received her first paycheck. She remembered making a personal budget as an assignment in her Life Skills class in high school, but now she was doing it for real. She smiled to herself—she liked being a grownup.

Fortunately, Ryan was at Little Lambs when Sarah arrived and she could share her good news with him and Dawn at the same time. When Sarah had finished, Ryan said, "You have a fairly realistic idea about the amount of money you'll need for your move. We're not real busy now so I can take you to the credit union and see if we can set you up with a short-term loan."

"Thanks. I won't let you down," Sarah promised as she reached for her coat. "I'll make sure I make my payments on time every month."

After returning to the Children's Center, Sarah could scarcely keep her mind on what needed to be done. She kept imagining what it would be like having Charity with her all the time. While all the children were playing, Dawn suggested, "Why don't you use the phone in the lounge and call your mother. I know she'll be anxious to hear your good news."

It didn't take much encouragement for Sarah to hurry and dial the familiar number. Knowing this was her day off work, Sarah waited impatiently until her mother answered. "Hello, Mom," she nearly shouted as soon as she heard her mother's voice. "I got a job in Missoula. It's at Quality Computers and I start June fifth."

"Congratulations," Doris Brown replied, "but please slow down. You're so excited I can scarcely understand you. When are you planning to move?"

"I'm so busy with classes that I won't be able to go over until after graduation," Sarah explained. "Ryan Reynolds co-signed a loan for me so I could have enough money to get an apartment."

"Since Mark and I were planning to come for your graduation, maybe we could leave for Missoula right afterwards and help you go apartment hunting," Doris suggested. "I have several vacation days I haven't used and we could make this into a nice family vacation. It might be the last one we'll be able to have together."

Sarah was bursting with joy at her mother's obvious pride. How different their relationship had become from what it had been five years earlier. "That sounds like a lot of fun," she exclaimed. "Jeff was planning to come for my graduation. Maybe between the two cars, I can get all my stuff to Missoula and I won't have to rent a trailer or pickup."

"I'm so proud of you, Sarah," Doris Brown exclaimed. "You've worked extremely hard to get yourself out of a bad situation, and I'm sure you'll be able to handle whatever challenge befalls you."

❧

June fifth, Sarah awoke early in her furnished apartment in Missoula. Jeff had been able to convince a landlord to hold the cute little place until Sarah and her mother were able to come to Missoula to check it out. It was a basic, one-bedroom apartment, perfect for a single, working woman. Sarah planned where she would put Charity's bed, toys, and all her adaptive equipment. She scanned the morning newspaper for a possible day care for her daughter. She noticed one connected with the University that specialized in disabled children. The only problem was, she did not have a car to drive the five miles there.

At 8:30, Sarah locked the door to her apartment and walked the four blocks to her new job. On the one hand, she could scarcely contain her excitement, but on the other, a sense of nervousness enveloped her. She questioned if she was up to the challenge.

Upon arriving at Quality Computers, Sarah went directly to Eric Johnson's office. "Welcome to Quality Computers," the manager greeted as he extended his right hand. "We're privileged to have someone with your qualifications join our business."

Sarah blushed as she murmured, "Thank you."

"The first thing we have to do is take care of the boring paperwork," the manager stated. "The bad part is that most of it we can't do on computer, but have to use old fashioned pen and paper."

Sarah filled in forms and read insurance agreements for nearly an hour. When she was finished, Eric led her to the repair room in the back, introduced her to her coworkers and showed her where the various parts and diagnostic tools were kept. The store manager finally showed Sarah where her workstation would be and already had a computer there for her to repair.

Within a half hour, Sarah had her first computer passing all the diagnostic tests, much to the amazement of the other technicians. For lunch, while the others went to a nearby restaurant, Sarah ate a simple peanut butter sandwich, apple, and chips in the employee lounge. She was so eager to get back to her next assignment that she returned to work twenty minutes early.

Sarah scarcely noticed the time until ten minutes past five when she heard Jeff Blair's voice in the front, asking for her. She immediately cleared her work area and joined him. "Would you like to stop for dinner on the way home?" he asked as he held the front door open for her, his cane in his right hand. "There's a real cute place just down the block."

"I'd enjoy that," Sarah replied. "I am pretty tired."

Throughout their meal, the couple centered their discussion on the air pollution in Missoula and how irritating it can become for those with breathing problems. "I don't understand why Missoula has so much smog compared to other Montana cities," Sarah queried. "Isn't this supposed to be Big Sky Country?"

"We've been plagued with air quality problems as long as I can remember," Jeff replied. "When the air conditions are right, the smog gets trapped in the valley and isn't able to rise above the bordering mountain peaks. That's why as soon as I can afford it, I want to move out of town, away from the smog."

Through their meal, the couple kept their discussion on local Missoula issues. However, over dessert, their conversation became more personal. Jeff reached across the table and took her hand. "Sarah, we've come through so much together," he began, "and through it all, I've come to realize how much I love you." Jeff paused as he gazed lovingly into her eyes. "I would like to spend the rest of my life with you. Will you marry me?"

Tears welled in Sarah's eyes. She had long hoped that someday she and Jeff would marry, but she wanted to make sure he wanted her because of a mature love and not merely because he was the father of her child. Now she was sure Jeff loved her, in spite of what happened in the past. "Of course, I'll marry you," Sarah cried. "I've loved you for so long, but there always seemed to be a huge mountain separating us."

"You've crossed that mountain, both literally and figuratively," Jeff reminded her. "Now all we need to do is work out the details."

"First of all we need to have Charity here with us, instead of in Rocky Bluff," Sarah stated firmly. "I'll need to find a good day care for her before I can get her."

"I called the University Day Care today and there will be an opening for a disabled child the first of July," Jeff said. "They also said they had a special van they use to pick up handicapped children. Would you like to stop by there tomorrow after work and talk with them?"

Sarah beamed. Jeff was acting more and more like a father with each passing day. "Of course," she replied. "What I like best about that particular day care is that it's where students majoring in special education are trained. Charity would have the best experience possible there—excited young teachers, experienced supervisors, and cutting-edge technology to help her be her best."

❧

As soon as Sarah was done with work on the Friday before the long Fourth of July weekend, she hurried home and began packing a small suitcase. Early in the morning, she and Jeff were going to leave for Rocky Bluff to bring Charity back with them. She had just received her first paycheck, paid her rent, and written out a check for her loan to the Rocky Bluff Credit Union.

After dinner, she and Jeff went to the mall to get a few remaining items they needed for their daughter. The young couple strolled through the expensive children's stores.

"Isn't this adorable?" Sarah cooed as she took a pink lace dress from the rack.

Jeff nodded in agreement and instinctively reached for the

price tag and laughed. "I think it will be a long time before we'll be able to dress Charity in that."

Sarah shrugged her shoulders and sighed. "The best we can do right now are thrift store specials, but I've seen some pretty cute things there. It's just fun to dream."

After they wearied of walking the mall, Jeff and Sarah decided to stop at the food court before returning home. While they sipped their soft drinks, Jeff said softly, "I still have an entire year before I graduate. I don't think I can stand to wait until then to get married."

Sarah looked deep into his eyes. "I don't want to wait a year myself. I know money will be tight, but with the salary from your part-time job and my salary, if we live frugally, I'm sure we can make it. Besides, it would be so much better if both of us shared in Charity's care."

Jeff beamed as he squeezed her hand. "Since we both feel the same way shall we announce our engagement to the world?" he asked.

"I'd like to shout it so the entire world can hear," Sarah exclaimed excitedly. "Since we'll be in Rocky Bluff tomorrow, I'd like Dawn and Ryan to be the first to know."

"I can hardly wait to tell them," Jeff said and then paused as his eyes sparkled. "While we're in Rocky Bluff, why don't we ask Pastor Olson if he'll marry us over my Christmas break?"

Sarah could scarcely believe this was happening to her. Truly, her cup was overflowing with happiness. As soon as Dawn learned the young couple's plans, she could scarcely contain her excitement. "I know you won't be able to afford a large wedding," Dawn said, "but there'll be many in our church who would like to attend. I'm certain Teresa, Mother, and I can help you arrange an extremely nice wedding on a tight budget."

"But you've already done so much for us," Sarah protested weakly. "I can't expect you to do all that as well."

Dawn gave a teasing smirk. "Surely you won't deny us an opportunity to plan another celebration?" she said.

"If you put it in those terms, we'll just turn our wedding plans over to your willing hands," Sarah laughed. "In the meantime, we'll begin contacting our family and friends."

&

"Hello, Mickey," Jeff greeted as his birth father answered the telephone. "This is Jeff. I have some exciting news for you."

Mickey could scarcely believe his ears. It had been several weeks since he'd heard from his son, and he was becoming concerned that perhaps Jeff did not want to be a part of his life, after all. "Hi, Jeff," he replied. "What's going on?"

"Remember how I told you that the reason I wanted to know my medical background was because I was interested in some-day getting married and having a family?" Jeff responded.

"How could I ever forget," Mickey teased. "Who is the lucky girl?"

Jeff's voice became serious. "Her name is Sarah Brown. She's the mother of my daughter, Charity. Sarah got a job here in Missoula, and last weekend we drove to Rocky Bluff and brought our daughter back with us. We plan to be married over Christmas break."

"Congratulations, Jeff. I'm extremely proud of you. Not only for what you've done but whom you introduced me to."

Jeff was perplexed. He knew that while he was in Spokane he hadn't introduced Mickey to anyone, not even his father, Dan Blair. "Whom did I introduce you to?"

"You gave me a Bible and introduced me to Jesus Christ," Mickey explained. "I didn't realize it at the time, but that was the very thing I'd been looking for my entire life."

"I. . .I. . .I don't know what to say," Jeff stammered. "I'm so happy for you. I can hardly wait to tell my mom and dad. They'll be delighted."

Mickey became silent. He thought of all the wild, wicked things he had done in his life. His years in jail did not remove his guilt, but the Good News brought to him by his own son whom he'd given up for adoption had provided him with a peace he'd never known before. "I have a lot of restitution to make for all my misdeeds, especially for those I've harmed. Do you think your mother would be willing to see me so that I can ask her forgiveness for all the pain I caused in her life?"

"I'm certain my parents will grant you their forgiveness," Jeff replied. "Would you like to come to Missoula?"

"I'd like that very much," Mickey replied. "I'll have to check my work schedule, but I think I might be able to come the Labor Day weekend. Do you think that would be a good time?"

"Of course, I'll have to check with my parents, but I don't think they have anything planned. I'll call you back this weekend and let you know."

Mickey hesitated and then asked weakly, "If I do come, would it be possible to meet my granddaughter?"

fifteen

December 28, Sarah stood in a side room in the back of the Rocky Bluff Community Church, listening to the prelude music for her wedding. So much had happened since she had stood in the same room more than three-and-a half years before, waiting for Dawn Harkness to walk down the aisle to become Dawn Reynolds.

Charity was sitting in her wheelchair, dressed in a fancy new pink dress, holding a basket of rose petals in her lap. Dawn, who was the matron of honor, was busy straightening her husband's tie. In just a few minutes, Ryan would escort Sarah down the aisle where she was to become the bride of Jeff Blair.

Jeff's parents, Beth and Dan Blair, had just been ushered into the sanctuary, followed closely by his younger sister, Edith. Although the church had been completely remodeled, this church was the same one the Blairs had been married in many years before. At that moment, all of Sarah's life seemed to come together in a sense of fulfillment and joy.

Sarah's mother was beaming as she sat on the front row. Her tall, sixteen-year-old son, Mark, was beside her. During Mark's many visits to Rocky Bluff Community College, he had decided that he, too, would like to attend RBCC as well. Sarah had been the first person in their family to go to college, but as he watched what his sister had accomplished he figured—*If she can do it, so can I.*

In the far back of the church, a distinguished looking man sat by himself, smiling with joy. This was the first time Mickey

Kilmer had been back in Rocky Bluff since he had kidnapped his son, Jeffey, away from the boy's unwed mother. If any person had made a dramatic change in his life, it was Mickey. Since becoming a Christian, Mickey had asked forgiveness from Beth and Dan for the heartache he had caused them. He was now sitting in the same church at the same time as the police officers and attorneys who worked the case against him. All were there as redeemed sinners celebrating the marriage and miracles in the lives of Sarah Brown, Jeff Blair, and little Charity.

Sarah spotted Jay and Angie Harkness sitting near the front of the church with their three children and her mother, Mitzi Quinata. As her college instructor and advisor, Jay had helped her over many difficult periods of discouragement and frustrations. He was obviously aglow with the satisfaction of seeing another student of his make a success of her life.

Nancy Harkness, Jay and Dawn's mother, had just completed the final details for the gala reception that was to follow. Even though her steps were beginning to slow, Nancy was the first one that people in Rocky Bluff called upon whenever there was a social event that needed expert planning. Sarah had always admired the many talents of the matriarch of the community.

Ryder Long and Vanessa White were sitting in the middle of the church holding hands. A bright diamond ring adorned Vanessa's hand. Both had returned from the University of Iowa to spend Christmas with their families. Neither one wanted to miss the wedding of their college friend and dreamed of the day they, too, would be saying their vows at the altar.

Teresa Olson had brought Rebecca Hatfield from the nursing home. Rebecca was dressed in a new dress and smiled sweetly to everyone, but her eyes were blank with confusion. However, when she saw Sarah walk down the aisle, a flicker of connection entered her eyes. Somewhere, under the worn-out body and mind, the spirit of Rebecca Hatfield was as strong and loving as ever.

Sarah's eyes blended into Jeff's as she walked down the aisle on Ryan Reynolds's arm. Whether they had had a child out of wedlock or not, Sarah was certain their love was so strong that they still would be marrying each other. As they spoke their wedding vows, Sarah and Jeff's eyes did not leave each other's until they closed them in prayer. Truly, this marriage was founded on the love and forgiveness of Jesus Christ.

When Pastor Olson raised his hand to give the traditional wedding blessing, he added something personal for the unique situation.

"Rocky Bluff is not only a place, it is a state of mind," he reminded them. "Rocky Bluff is not only a town in Montana, but it can be any place where people still share the love of Jesus Christ with those around them. The ideals of Rocky Bluff are based on a loving community, and I pray that we all might take them with us wherever our individual paths may lead. Let us all be assured that those who know and believe in Jesus Christ will someday be together again in a place far better than our mountain home of Rocky Bluff, Montana."

A Letter To Our Readers

Dear Reader:

In order that we might better contribute to your reading enjoyment, we would appreciate your taking a few minutes to respond to the following questions. We welcome your comments and read each form and letter we receive. When completed, please return to the following:

Rebecca Germany, Fiction Editor
Heartsong Presents
PO Box 719
Uhrichsville, Ohio 44683

1. Did you enjoy reading *Love Abounds?*
   ☐ Very much. I would like to see more books
      by this author!
   ☐ Moderately
      I would have enjoyed it more if _____

      _____

      _____

2. Are you a member of **Heartsong Presents**? Yes ☐ No ☐
   If no, where did you purchase this book?_____

   _____

3. How would you rate, on a scale from 1 (poor) to 5 (superior), the cover design?_____

4. On a scale from 1 (poor) to 10 (superior), please rate the following elements.

   _____ Heroine   _____ Plot

   _____ Hero   _____ Inspirational theme

   _____ Setting   _____ Secondary characters

5. These characters were special because_____

_____

_____

6. How has this book inspired your life?_____

_____

_____

7. What settings would you like to see covered in future
   Heartsong Presents books?_____

_____

_____

8. What are some inspirational themes you would like to see
   treated in future books?_____

_____

_____

9. Would you be interested in reading other **Heartsong
   Presents** titles?   Yes ❑   No ❑

10. Please check your age range:
    ❑ Under 18   ❑ 18-24   ❑ 25-34
    ❑ 35-45   ❑ 46-55   ❑ Over 55

11. How many hours per week do you read?_____

Name _____

Occupation _____

Address _____

City _____ State _____ Zip _____

Reunions

The spark of love stands the test of time and is fanned to a flame as four couples are reunited. These contemporary novellas include four reunion celebrations—high school, college, family, and organ donors—that will tug at the tightest of heartstrings.

paperback, 352 pages, 5 ⁹⁄₁₆" x 8"

····Heart♥ng····

Any 12
Heartsong
Presents titles
for only
$26.95 *

CONTEMPORARY ROMANCE IS CHEAPER BY THE DOZEN!

Buy any assortment of twelve *Heartsong Presents* titles and save 25% off of the already discounted price of $2.95 each!

*plus $2.00 shipping and handling per order and sales tax where applicable.

HEARTSONG PRESENTS *TITLES AVAILABLE NOW:*

(If ordering from this page, please remember to include it with the order form.)

·······Presents·······

Great Inspirational Romance at a Great Price!

Heartsong Presents books are inspirational romances in contemporary and historical settings, designed to give you an enjoyable, spirit-lifting reading experience. You can choose wonderfully written titles from some of today's best authors like Veda Boyd Jones, Yvonne Lehman, Tracie Peterson, Andrea Boeshaar, and many others.

When ordering quantities less than twelve, above titles are $2.95 each.
Not all titles may be available at time of order.

Hearts♥ng Presents
Love Stories Are Rated G!

That's for godly, gratifying, and of course, great! If you love
thrilling love story, but don't appreciate the sordidness of som
popular paperback romances, **Heartsong Presents** is for you. I
fact, **Heartsong Presents** is the *only inspirational romance boo
club* featuring love stories where Christian faith is the primar
ingredient in a marriage relationship.

Sign up today to receive your first set of four, never befor
published Christian romances. Send no money now; you wi
receive a bill with the first shipment. You may cancel at any tin
without obligation, and if you aren't completely satisfied wi
any selection, you may return the books for an immediate refun

Imagine. . .four new romances every four weeks—two hi
torical, two contemporary—with men and women like you wh
long to meet the one God has chosen as the love of their lives.
all for the low price of $9.97 postpaid.

To join, simply complete the coupon below and mail to t
address provided. **Heartsong Presents** romances are rated G f
another reason: They'll arrive *Godspeed!*
